'I'm not afraid to kiss you,' Gwenyth said, shifting her position so that she could link her fingers behind Jeb's neck.

Her gaze slipped to the firm but sensual line of his mouth. Her heart was suddenly thudding, but she couldn't draw back now. Bravado demanded that she continue with what she had begun. Her lashes fluttering down, she placed her lips lightly against his. Jeb's hands moved to her waist, holding her, yet making no attempt to pull her closer as she kissed each corner of his mouth.

Feeling as though she'd played with danger long enough, she let her hands fall from his neck. In a voice that was lightly scathing, if not quite as steady as she'd have liked, she murmured, 'Have I proved my point?'

'Now I'll prove mine.'

ARROGANT INVADER

BY

JENNY ARDEN

MILLS & BOON LIMITED
ETON HOUSE   18–24 PARADISE ROAD
RICHMOND   SURREY   TW9 1SR

*First published in Great Britain 1990
by Mills & Boon Limited*

© Jenny Arden 1990

*Australian copyright 1990
Philippine copyright 1990
This edition 1990*

ISBN 0 263 76806 6

*Set in 10 on 12 pt Linotron Palatino
01-9009-48753
Typeset in Great Britain by Centracet, Cambridge
Made and printed in Great Britain*

CHAPTER ONE

SUNLIGHT gleamed on the aircraft's broad wing as Gwenyth leaned forward to look out at the massed furrow of low cloud below her which stretched away into the distance. The fact that the plane would probably land and taxi to a halt in steady rain didn't lessen her sense of excitement. She had loved every minute of the year she had spent in Aix-en-Provence, studying at the university there, but suddenly she realised how much she had missed the weather-swept mountains of North Wales.

Impulsively she turned to her companion and then checked what she had been going to say as she saw that Marc was dozing. She settled back in her seat, a tender glow in her amber eyes as her gaze lingered on her fiancé.

When she had first met him six months ago, her initial impression had been that he was too charming and polished to be sincere. The several dozen roses, in various shades, which had arrived at her flat the following day had failed to impress her, although she had thanked him nicely for them.

Nor had the high position he held in the foreign exchange section of one of the international banks, nor his family's estate at St Remy, cut much ice with her. Marc Brassac might be rich and influential, but so was her family and, more importantly, one of her father's favourite maxims was that it paid to judge a man not by who he was, but by what he was.

Since Marc was used to taking his pick where women were concerned, he had been a shade nonplussed when, despite the gentlemanly ardour with which he had been courting her, she had failed to fall into his arms. Challenged, he had set about winning her with a tenacity and determination which had eventually convinced her that his attentions were serious.

She glanced at the solitaire diamond that sparkled on her engagement finger. She liked being in charge of her own destiny, and it gave her a secure feeling to know that she hadn't been swept off her feet. Instead, her love for Marc had grown steadily out of a romantic friendship.

The drone of the aircraft's engines altered in pitch, and a few moments later a voice announced over the intercom that the plane was beginning its descent towards Manchester Airport and that passengers should extinguish their cigarettes and fasten their seatbelts. Gwenyth put a gentle hand on her fiancé's arm.

'Marc, wake up. We'll be landing soon.'

Drawing a deep breath, he flickered his eyes open. He shook his head slightly as though making an effort to rouse himself. 'I didn't realise I'd gone to sleep,' he said, giving her a smile as he pressed the button in the arm-rest of his seat to bring the back upright. 'It's a habit acquired on business trips.'

'I haven't travelled as much as you have,' she answered. 'I still find flying a thrill.'

'That's what I love about you.' Marc took her hand and carried it to his lips. 'You have such a zest for life.'

'I love you, too,' she murmured.

They exchanged a warm glance as the noise of the engines increased to a thunderous roar. From out of the window the minute buildings grew larger and the roads wider. There was a slight jar as the plane's wheels touched and then rolled along the runway, the powerful slipstream sending long waves rippling through the grass at the side of the tarmac.

The aircraft taxied to a halt by the terminal building and Marc stood up to get their hand-luggage from where he had stowed it in an overhead locker. Glancing out of the cabin window, he remarked with rueful humour, 'It's not very welcoming, is it?'

His foreign accent was attractive, and through his work at the bank he was as fluent in her language as she was in his.

'Whenever I fly into Manchester it always seems to rain,' Gwenyth observed with a smile.

'*Tiens*, a typical English summer!' Marc joked.

She laughed and protested, 'It doesn't rain all the time. It'll probably brighten up in an hour or so, but even in the rain the drive from Chester to Bron-y-Foel is beautiful.'

Joining the queue of passengers who stood waiting in the aisle to disembark, they were soon off the plane and heading along the glass-walled corridor of the airport terminal. They made an attractive couple, Marc several inches taller than she was, his dark good looks the perfect foil for her porcelain colouring and cloud of chestnut hair that turned men's heads.

'Who'll be at the airport to meet us?' Marc enquired as, having come through Passport Control, they collected their luggage and proceeded towards Customs.

'Just Dad, I expect,' she answered.

His brows came together quizzically. 'How's that?'

'Well, Mother will want to have dinner ready and——'

Realising that she'd misinterpreted his question, Marc cut in, 'No, what I meant was, I didn't think your father could drive. You said he was. . .disabled.' The English word eluded him for a moment.

'He is,' Gwenyth confirmed, 'but he can still drive. His car has all the controls on the steering column.'

'Ah, yes. Of course.' Marc nodded. 'I should have realised.'

'It's surprising how mobile Dad is,' Gwenyth told him. 'Despite the accident he's not confined completely to a wheelchair. He gets about too, although with some difficulty, with the aid of callipers and crutches.'

'It sounds as if he's made an amazing adjustment.'

A note of quiet pride in her voice, she answered simply, 'My father's a very determined man.'

With nothing to declare, they quickly emerged into the large arrivals hall. Their plane had arrived on schedule, and she was about to remark that her father must have been delayed when she suddenly recognised Jeb Hunter. A prickle of antipathy ran up her spine. She disliked the man on several counts— the main one being that he was cold and ruthless.

Three years ago the Brynteg Quarries, which had been owned by her father, had been in the process of opening up two new chambers at the cost of a quarter of a million pounds. The financial gamble would have undoubtedly paid off if her father hadn't been seriously injured in a rock fall while he had been inspecting the work that had been in progress.

But with him recovering slowly in hospital, the company had quickly begun to run into cash-flow problems.

Concerned about what would happen not just to his employees, but to the whole economy of the local area if the Brynteg Quarries were to close, he had decided to accept the offer of a take-over. Gwenyth had protested, but he had been adamant.

'The only way I can save the company is by selling the controlling interest in it. Things would be different if I were fit, but the fact is I'm in a wheelchair and likely to remain in one.'

'Dad, you don't know that for certain,' she had answered, her throat tight.

Her father had patted her hand. 'But I do know one thing. The quarries need to be run by a man who's determined to increase output, and who'll drive himself as hard to achieve that goal as he will the people who work for him. Jeb Hunter's shrewd and dynamic. He allows nothing to come between him and success. He'll do more than make the quarries pay. He'll make the company expand and diversify, and meanwhile I'll still be a shareholder and have a seat on the board.'

Gwenyth hadn't argued any more, but her father's opinion of Jeb Hunter hadn't altered her own. She knew that he had a reputation for ruthlessness in business, and the way he had approached her father with a take-over bid so soon after the accident which had left him crippled put her in mind of a shark scenting blood from afar.

To avoid casually bumping into him she would have looked away quickly and hoped that, among so many people, he hadn't seen her. But it was too late.

Their eyes met, and without hesitation he strode up to where she was standing with Marc.

Six feet tall, urbane and yet rugged with it, he had an inborn air of command. Even the way he held his dark head spoke of someone accustomed to authority. The jutting line of his jaw complemented his straight nose and his cheekbones that were as proud as a Comanche's. His mouth was sensuous and as masculine as the rest of him. It could look cruel, especially when his blue eyes narrowed—as they often did.

He was evidently at the airport to meet a client, for he was wearing a charcoal-grey suit, white shirt and Paisley silk tie. His immaculate appearance emphasised that he was a man to be reckoned with.

Despite her animosity towards him she steeled herself to be polite. 'Hello, Jeb,' she began.

She thought she did it rather well, her tone cool yet friendly, but the amused glitter in his eyes told her that he wasn't deceived. It annoyed her that Jeb seemed able to read her like a book, especially when, to please her father, she had always made an effort to hide her dislike of the man.

'Hello, Gwenyth,' he answered. 'Welcome home.'

To her complete surprise, as he spoke he put a capable hand on her shoulder and bent to kiss her. It was no more than a brush of his lips against her cheek, but for an instant she felt completely off balance and shatteringly aware of his sexual magnetism.

Immediately her temper flared, her amber eyes sparking as she looked up at him. She didn't want Jeb to kiss her, even in the most casual way. Other women might enjoy succumbing to his virile charisma, but she wasn't one of them. He knew perfectly well that she liked to keep him at arm's length.

A sardonic smile touched the corners of his mouth as he saw the tinge of indignant colour that had come into her face, but his voice was bland as he asked, 'Did you have a good flight?'

She drew a deep breath, checking her temper. She had been scrupulously polite to Jeb Hunter whenever their paths had crossed for three years. She wasn't going to ruin that record now.

'Yes, thank you. Everything's been fine,' she answered with forced calm.

'I hope you haven't been waiting long. The traffic was very heavy approaching the airport.'

'You mean. . .?' She faltered in sudden comprehension. 'You mean you're here to meet me? But why? Where's Dad?'

'He's gashed his leg. When he rang me, your mother was about to drive him to Casualty.'

'Is it serious?' Gwenyth asked in concern.

'No, but he wasn't sure how long they'd keep him at the hospital. He knew I was in Manchester today visiting the factory so, to be on the safe side, he asked me if I'd meet you,' Jeb explained. He turned his attention to Marc, his quick appraising gaze missing not one detail of her fiancé's dapper attire. 'And who's this?' he enquired.

His tone was genial, but Gwenyth knew him too well to miss the slight edge of derision in it. Refusing to let it irritate her, she answered, 'This is Marc Brassac, my fiancé.' She tucked her hand through Marc's arm in the mute assertion that she belonged to him, and went on, 'Marc, I'd like you to meet Jeb Hunter, a business associate of my father's.'

'I'm pleased to meet you, Mr Hunter,' Marc said smoothly.

For an instant Gwenyth thought there was a chilly glint in the depths of Jeb's blue eyes. But she had obviously imagined it, for his voice was lazy as he commented, as he and Marc shook hands, 'So, congratulations are in order.'

'Thank you.' Marc answered for both of them.

Together they had a lot of luggage. Taking two of the smart tan suitcases off the overloaded trolley, Jeb remarked, 'Your father didn't mention he was meeting the two of you. Does he know you're engaged?'

'Marc only proposed to me last week,' Gwenyth said as they made their way towards the exit.

'With her stay in France coming to an end, I wasn't going to risk losing her,' Marc explained, giving her a smile. 'I tried to persuade her to let her parents know to expect us both, but she insisted on surprising them.'

Jeb made no comment, yet Gwenyth was left with the distinct impression that he found their behaviour vaguely childish. A flash of annoyance went through her. She and Marc weren't a pair of teenagers in love with love. She was twenty-one and Marc was twenty-eight, only four years younger than Jeb. In any case, their romance was no affair of his.

The rain was falling more heavily now and she turned the collar of her jacket up as they left the airport terminal. She was glad that Jeb's dark red Range Rover was parked handily. He promptly unlocked the front passenger door and, his hand at her elbow, he put her into the car before she could demur and say that she'd rather sit with Marc.

When the luggage had been loaded in the boot he slid behind the wheel, while Marc got in the back. As he started the ignition she flicked a glance at him. The rain had darkened the raven thickness of his hair, making it unruly in a sensual sort of way. Her lips tightened slightly. Jeb's saturnine looks had never appealed to her. His hawkish eyes only had to clash with hers for her to feel strangely challenged, and what was more, she thought with antagonism, he seemed to know it and to be amused by her reaction.

He pulled out into the traffic and then asked, 'Which part of France are you from, Mr Brassac?'

'I live in Aix and have done for the past two years. Before that I worked abroad in our offices in Zurich.'

'You move about with your job, then.'

'The bank likes us to get as much experience of different markets as we can,' Marc said with faint arrogance. 'I've also been to our New York offices several times, and to Tokyo.'

'Really.' Jeb's tone was polite if a shade dry.

'What line of work are you in?' Marc enquired.

'I run the slate quarries at Bron-y-Foel.'

'He took over from Dad three years ago,' Gwenyth explained.

Jeb's gaze swung to her briefly, knowledge in his blue eyes. His voice pitched too low for Marc in the back of the Range Rover to be able to catch what he said, he jibed, 'Still resenting me, Gwenyth?'

Had they been alone together, she might have given in to the strong temptation to flash back with an answer. As it was, she remained silent. The masculine line of Jeb's mouth quirked into a cynically amused smile, as though he knew exactly what her restraint cost her.

'Am I right in thinking that although you run the quarries you're not Welsh?' Marc asked. 'Your accent sounds English to me.'

'Yes, I'm English,' Jeb confirmed. 'And, as such, although my home's now in Bron-y-Foel, I'm still referred to locally as the foreigner.'

'Then there's not much hope for me.' Marc laughed.

'None at all,' Jeb agreed. 'To distinguish between the two of us, you'll be spoken of, I expect, as the foreign foreigner.'

'That won't worry me,' Gwenyth told him, unappreciative of his prediction. 'And I'm sure it won't worry Marc.'

'Then he's different from me,' Jeb answered, 'because I intend to be accepted eventually.'

'There's not a chance,' she returned with a touch of malice. 'You were christened the foreigner when you arrived and, since you don't speak Welsh and don't have any family ties in Bron-y-Foel, you'll always be an outsider.'

A lazy glint in his blue eyes, he said, 'So you think family ties would make a difference?'

'They might,' she conceded reluctantly, 'if you were to marry someone local.'

'I'll keep the suggestion in mind,' he promised.

He sounded serious, and curiosity forced her to glance at him. His chiselled features told her nothing and she looked away again, wondering whose name his was currently linked with. Cross with herself, she cut the speculation short. It was of no interest to her who he was dating.

They had left the outskirts of the city behind, when Jeb asked casually, 'When's the wedding?'

'We haven't set a date yet,' she told him.

'But we'd like to be married soon,' Marc put in. 'We know each other well, so there's no need to have a long engagement.'

'What about finishing your degree?' Jeb queried.

Had she not met Marc she would have certainly taken her finals next summer. But he wasn't keen on the idea of her returning to Aberystwyth University in September.

'If I continue with the course,' she answered, 'Marc and I will be apart for almost a whole year.'

'I can't see that as a problem. Absence is supposed to make the heart grow fonder,' Jeb commented.

She resented his interference, but, before she could reply that she didn't need his advice in order to make up her mind, Marc stated, 'Gwenyth won't need to work after we're married, so I can't see any point in her finishing her degree.'

Jeb flicked a glance at her. 'What *will* you be doing, then?' he asked, mild derision in his tone as he added, 'Raising little Brassacs?'

'In time,' she almost snapped at him. Unable to understand why she was letting him get under her skin, she went on, 'Meanwhile, Marc entertains a lot, and I'll have the house to run.'

'I thought you were very keen to have a career of some kind,' Jeb said with an edge of mockery.

'That was before I fell in love with Marc.'

'I'm surprised you don't feel you owe it to your

father to take your degree when he's kept you at
university for three years,' Jeb observed.

'Dad won't push me to go on for a fourth year if I
don't want to.' But he would be very disappointed.
She knew that.

'Well, if you think it's fair to him. . .' With a shrug
Jeb let his sentence trail off, dismissing the subject
while making it perfectly clear what he thought about
it.

'And how fair were *you*, when you bought the
quarries?' she demanded accusingly.

A smile that had little to do with mirth lifted the
corners of his firm mouth. 'It's taken you a long time
to come out and say it, hasn't it?' he baited softly.

She flushed with annoyance and murmured, 'Then
doubtless you'll understand why I don't want you
preaching to me about what's fair.'

'If I hadn't bought the Brynteg Quarries, your
father's company would have been wound up by
now,' Jeb said bluntly.

Her amber eyes blazed, but she didn't answer. The
rhythmic flick of the windscreen wipers continued
as, for the next hour, the rain poured down without
a sign of stopping. The rolling border country gave
way gradually to a more rugged landscape. After the
bright glare of a Provençale summer, it seemed more
than ever Merlin's country, the summits of the
brooding mountains shrouded in mist and mystery.

'It's very austere, isn't it?' Marc commented on the
grim grandeur of the scenery.

Gwenyth glanced over her shoulder to chide
laughingly, 'That's part of its charm. Anyway, when
the sun shines the mountains look very different,
and some of the walks locally are really lovely.'

'I don't think Marc's the outdoor type,' Jeb made the comment as he shifted the Range Rover down a gear.

As it happened, his observation was correct. Marc was much more of a city person than she was. What annoyed her was the way Jeb made it sound like a criticism of her fiancé's masculinity.

At the head of the next sharp bend in the road Bron-y-Foel came into sight, set amid a vast amphitheatre of blue-tinted ranges. Against a soft pastel sky only a drift of stubborn cloud remained to veil one distant summit.

'You get a good view from here,' Jeb stated. 'There's a lay-by just ahead. If you like I'll pull in and you can get out for a minute.'

The air was fragrant after the rain, smelling of earth and heather. With her hand entwined in Marc's she pointed out some of the landmarks below them, while Jeb waited by the Range Rover.

The town that nestled between the slopes was pretty, especially with the sunlight gleaming on its wet roofs. Mountainous heaps of slate showed where the Brynteg Quarries had been hewn out of the hillside and yet, at the same time, melted into the charm of the dramatic valley.

As they returned to the car and stood for a moment before getting in, Marc asked Jeb, 'Is any use made of the mounds of slate?'

'It used to be all waste, but now a lot of it's crushed and used for motorway construction. Not that there's been any tipping externally at Brynteg for a number of years.'

'For conservation reasons, I suppose,' Marc guessed.

'Partly,' Jeb agreed, 'and partly because there's much less waste in slate quarrying these days. Forty years ago, for every sixty-seven tons of raw blocks that were produced, only one ton finished up as slabs. Most of the other sixty-six tons were dumped on tips. But with modern shearing machines on the rock face, and the cutting of blocks and slabs with diamond-impregnated saws, the waste ratio has been reduced now to about three to one.'

'That's a big improvement,' Marc commented. A high flier in the bank, anything relating to the world of finance always engaged his attention. 'What happens to the slate once it's produced?'

'Most of it goes to our manufacturing company, which is based in Manchester,' Jeb told him. 'There it's made into roofing material, window-sills, cladding and the like, before being distributed. The rest of it is sold direct by the quarry to other slate producers and merchants.'

'It sounds very interesting. Would it be possible for me to have a look round while I'm here?'

Jeb considered the request. As visitors who weren't at the quarry on business would only be a hindrance, Gwenyth expected him to refuse, but instead he stated, 'I haven't got too heavy a schedule tomorrow morning. If you drive into the quarry at ten and come to my office, I'll arrange for someone to take you round.'

'Fine,' Marc said, and then checked, 'Does that suit you, *chérie*?'

Since she had no time for Jeb Hunter, she would have much preferred to have kept well out of his way, but, as Marc specifically wanted to see the quarries, she pretended to be quite happy with the plan. 'Yes, that's fine,' she agreed.

Jeb's mouth curved with amusement and, nettled by his mockery, she turned away. The ground was uneven and, as she went to walk past him to get into the Range Rover, she tripped. Immediately he snatched hold of her arm to steady her. She was aware of the strength in his fingers and of the unaccountable quickening of her pulse.

'Careful!' he said sharply.

'I'm all right,' she insisted, unnerved by his closeness. He released her and, quickly recovering her poise, she added, 'Thanks.'

Yet she felt strangely shaken as they moved off again. Jeb's touch had been impersonal and automatic. There had been no need for her to have reacted as though she'd been burned by it.

She pushed the incident from her mind, determined not to let it bother her. They had only to cross the town and drive a short way up a steep slope and she would be home. She felt a tug of excitement with the thought.

Her sister, Sian, who was fourteen, must have been watching for the car, for the moment it drew up she came racing down the steps from the house with Ricky barking furiously at her heels. Jeb gave the Welsh collie a friendly pat as he came round the Range Rover to open Gwenyth's door for her, but, delighted to be home, she was already getting out.

The next few minutes were lost in a flurry of laughter with both Gwenyth and Sian talking at once. Excited by her arrival, Ricky ran backwards and forwards, jumping up first at her and then at Marc.

Sian, noticing the Frenchman for the first time, suddenly stopped chattering in Welsh and fell silent.

'Are you going to introduce your fiancé or shall I?' Jeb drawled.

'Fiancé?' Sian squeaked. At that moment her parents came out of the house. 'Mother, Dad, what do you know?' Sian called to them. 'Gwenyth's engaged!'

CHAPTER TWO

DEREC MORGAN manoeuvred his wheelchair down the ramp with practised ease, while his wife paused a moment, her face alight, before she hurried down the steps which led from the front door.

'Engaged!' she exclaimed, hugging her daughter. 'Did I hear right?'

'Yes, I'm engaged.' Gwenyth laughed.

'And to think we weren't at the airport to meet you!'

Good-temperedly her father said, 'We would have been, but you know how your mother fusses. She insisted I get my leg seen to at the hospital.'

'Quite right, too.' Gwenyth smiled as she kissed him.

She slipped her hand into her fiancé's and was on the point of introducing him, when her father stated, 'And this must be Marc.'

'Yes, this is Marc,' she confirmed. 'Darling, I'd like you to meet my parents. This is my mother, Catrin, and my father, Derec Morgan.'

'*Enchanté.*' Suave and charming, Marc shook hands with each of them.

'Gwenyth's mentioned you so often in her letters,' Catrin said warmly.

'I'm glad I haven't taken you completely by surprise,' Marc answered, 'though I must apologise for arriving like this without warning.'

'Nonsense,' Catrin insisted. 'We never stand on

ceremony. Visitors are always welcome. We're delighted to have you.'

'*Vous êtes très gentille, madame*, or may I call you Catrin?'

'Yes, of course. Please do.'

As her mother spoke, Gwenyth inadvertently glanced at Jeb, who was unloading the luggage from the Range Rover. The faint glitter of amused contempt she saw in his blue eyes told her what his opinion was of her fiancé's charm, sending a quicksilver dart of annoyance through her. Damn the man, she thought, cross that he could rile her merely with a derisive lift of his dark brows.

'We seem to be leaving all the work to Jeb,' Derec announced. 'Let's get the luggage inside.'

Jeb tucked a bulky holdall under one arm. Reaching for two of the suitcases, he glanced at Marc to ask, 'Can you manage the rest?'

Gwenyth saw her fiancé's mouth tighten slightly, as though he was aware that Jeb had taken charge of the heaviest luggage. 'You should have been a porter, Mr Hunter,' he commented.

'Cheers,' Jeb returned drily.

It was obvious from his reply that he hadn't intended Marc to take his question as an insult, but she didn't blame her fiancé for interpreting it as such. Jeb's whole manner seemed to imply that with Marc he was dealing with a lightweight.

Her mother suggested that the luggage be left for the time being at the foot of the stairs in the large hall. 'If we'd known about your engagement we'd have had a bottle of champagne to drink to the two of you,' she said when they were seated in the drawing-room.

'It's not too late to get some,' Derec stated promptly. 'We'll celebrate with champagne tonight.'

'Have you seen Gwen's ring yet?' Sian chirped in. 'It's a real sparkler!'

'I noticed the way it caught the sunlight in the garden,' her mother answered, 'but I'd like to see it close to.'

'Marc gave it to me the same evening that he proposed,' Gwenyth said.

She turned her head to smile at her fiancé, only to have her gaze intercepted by Jeb's sardonic blue stare.

'Did seeing the ring influence your answer?' he drawled.

'Oh, Jeb, don't be such a tease!' Her mother laughed.

Except, Gwenyth thought angrily, he wasn't teasing. He was deliberately baiting her. Generally she quelled the impulse to retaliate, but she had been the target for his sarcasm ever since he had met her at the airport, and the temptation was too great. Seeming to joke in return, she said, 'With a diamond as big as the Ritz, Jeb, I wouldn't marry you!'

'I haven't asked you,' he replied.

To her chagrin the others laughed.

'It's certainly a lovely ring,' her mother said. 'To choose a diamond cut in a heart-shape, you must be a romantic, Marc.'

'Where your daughter's concerned, I most definitely am.'

The conversation moved on, and Gwenyth, whose gaze had been clashing stormily with Jeb's, looked away. She wasn't going to let his mockery spoil her homecoming, not when she had so looked forward to it, and when Marc and her family seemed to have clicked immediately, just as she had hoped they would.

Some while later Marc commented, 'Gwenyth's been trying to teach me a few Welsh words. It's fascinating the way the place-names are so descriptive.'

'It's a great language,' her father responded, lighting his pipe. He drew on it and then, as he shook the match out and dropped it in the ashtray alongside him, he continued, 'All the place-names in Wales have meanings. Brynteg, for instance, which the quarry takes its name from, means beautiful hill.'

'We stopped to have a look at the view from there,' Marc said. 'It lives up to its name.'

'What's more, the place grows on you,' Jeb observed. 'I'd find it hard to have to leave Wales now.'

'You're becoming a stick in the mud, Jeb,' Gwenyth said, scoring a subtle dig at him in revenge for his mockery earlier.

'If I'm a stick in the mud after only three years here, what does that make you?' he returned.

It was the second time he had got the better of her effortlessly with his quick humour.

'Let me show you to your room so you can get unpacked, Marc,' Catrin said.

'It's all right, Mother,' Gwenyth said. 'I'm going upstairs, so I'll show him.'

She went ahead of him into the parquet-floored hall. Several fine-looking pot plants stood on the carved oak chest near the stairs and, seeing them, Marc asked, 'Who's the house-plant expert?'

'Mother is.'

As Gwenyth answered, Catrin came out of the drawing-room carrying some of the tea things.

'I've been admiring your plants,' Marc told her. 'Isn't this a stephanotis?'

His interest drew a pleased smile in response. 'It's a hoya,' Catrin said. 'The leaves are similar but the flowers are different. I do have a stephanotis, though. Come through into the conservatory and I'll show you——' She broke off, admonishing herself with a laugh. 'Goodness, what am I thinking of? After your journey you want to see your room, not be bored with my pot plants.'

'Not at all,' Marc insisted. 'I'd love to see them.'

At that moment the telephone in the hall rang.

'I'll get it,' Gwenyth announced.

The caller was Huw Davis, the transport manager at the quarries and a long-standing friend of her father's. 'Hello, Gwenyth,' he began, quick to recognise her voice. 'So you didn't decide to stay in France, then?'

'No, not this time.' She laughed. 'Do you want to speak to Dad?'

'As a matter of fact it's Jeb I'm trying to track down. Is he there?'

'Yes, I'll get him for you.'

Whatever the problem was that had cropped up, Jeb quickly dealt with it. He was a born leader, a man with few wasted words but plenty of charisma, she thought grudgingly as she went to the foot of the stairs to pick up her hand-luggage. When he issued orders, others automatically obeyed.

He rang off and strolled towards her. 'Tell me which suitcases are yours and I'll carry them upstairs for you,' he offered.

'They're all mine apart from the maroon one with the matching leather straps.'

'I should have guessed.'

It was infuriating how, with one brief comment, he could heap scorn on Marc's taste. Her amber eyes aglow with annoyance, she said coldly, 'I've had about enough of your sneering at my fiancé.'

'It's touching the way you're so quick to leap to his defence,' he mocked. 'Do you intend making a life-time habit of it?'

'I shan't have to,' she answered shortly, 'because luckily, in France, people have some manners.'

The masculine line of his mouth quirked with amusement, yet the glitter in his eyes was far from mirthful. Unable to understand why the hitherto low-key antagonism between them was suddenly causing sparks to fly, she turned and went up the staircase ahead of him, leading the way along the wide landing to her bedroom.

He followed her inside and set her suitcases down at the foot of her bed before glancing around. It was a pretty room. A cream carpet covered the expanse of floor, while the walls were white, setting off the dark wood furniture. Patterned curtains in Wedgwood blue matched the bedspread, while the same shade was picked up again in the sprigged cushion on the window-seat and the runner on the chest of drawers. The very feminine surroundings seemed to intensify his unsettling masculine presence.

'Blue and white,' he said, commenting on the décor. 'Very virginal and appropriate, I suppose— when you went away.'

'My relationship with my fiancé is my affair,' she flared. 'And so is the colour scheme of my bedroom!'

Hawkish eyes scrutinised her, taking in her angry blush. 'You don't like me much, do you?' he baited.

'I have no strong feeling about you one way or the other,' she said, shrugging.

'Liar.'

'Why ask if you know the answer?' she demanded, rising to his taunt in spite of herself.

Ignoring her question, he asked lazily, 'What is it you've got against me, apart from the fact that I've taken over from your father at the quarry? We're alone. You can be frank.'

On top of his hateful sarcasm, he was implying that she was insincere. Both to prove him wrong and to satisfy her simmering temper, she retorted, 'All right. I'll be frank. I don't like you because you're hard and ruthless and you manipulate people. Everything you do has an ulterior motive, and the only thing that interests you is profit. In short, you're inhuman.'

Jeb's gaze raked her with slow thoroughness, moving from her perfect features over her slim figure before returning to her face again. 'What makes you think I'm not human?' he enquired, a sensual note to his voice.

He hadn't touched her and yet the hot shiver that traced over her skin meant that it seemed as though he had. With the caress of his unfathomable blue eyes he had undressed her, exploring her body with leisurely masculine approval.

For an instant she stared back at him, feeling as if the breath had been knocked out of her. An electric awareness charged the air and, in a flurry of agitation, she turned away, not wanting him to see the warmth that was rising to her cheeks.

'I hate Dad to be reminded that he's limited in what he can do,' she said, staggered that, although her heart was beating rapidly, she sounded cool and composed. 'So would you mind bringing Marc's luggage upstairs as well as my other suitcase?'

'OK, just show me where he's sleeping.'

'In the room almost opposite mine,' she said, moving to the door to indicate it to him.

'Convenient,' he commented.

Veiled temper sparkled in her eyes, but she didn't demand that he explain what he meant by that. He was standing very close, too close, her senses told her, and she didn't want to tangle with him.

Jeb strode out of her bedroom and, in a burst of angry energy, she unzipped her suitcase and began to unpack, trying to push the sensual way he had studied her out of her mind. No man had ever looked at her that way before. It bordered on the insulting, as though, she thought furiously, he was judging her as a potential candidate for his harem. She was certain he had done it deliberately to shatter her cool poise. If so, it had had the desired effect. The knowledge added fuel to the fire of her dislike of him.

The top drawer of the Victorian mahogany chest of drawers near the window always stuck a little. She was trying to open it when Jeb returned.

'Can you manage?' he asked.

'Yes, of course.'

But despite the sharp tug she gave it as she answered, the drawer obstinately refused to budge. Jeb moved towards her and, without her knowing why, her heart began to knock against her ribs. Unsettled by his nearness, she moved quickly aside.

He opened the drawer for her and then ran his hand along the wooden edge to find out where it had been sticking.

'Rub it with some candle wax,' he advised. 'That should make it run smoothly.'

'I don't want to get wax marks on my best lingerie.'

Her unappreciative reply drew his gaze to the filmy garments she was holding and, wishing she hadn't spoken, she shoved them quickly in the drawer, dropping a silky camisole as she did so in her haste.

It fell at his feet. He picked it up and remarked, 'I'm surprised you bothered to pack all your things.'

'Why shouldn't I have?' she demanded, snatching the camisole out of his hand.

'It seems rather pointless to bring everything home when you're not staying.'

'I may be home another year yet,' she told him.

'I thought the aim was to duck out of your finals.'

'Well, you're wrong,' she snapped. 'I haven't decided yet what to do about finishing my degree. But for your information, ducking out of things isn't my style.'

His masculine mouth was a cynical line. 'I can't think of any other reason why you've got engaged to Marc.'

'The reason I'm marrying Marc is because I love him!' she flashed.

His gaze noted the indignant rise and fall of her breasts and the amber sparks in her eyes. There was a little charged silence and then he pronounced, 'You weren't meant for Marc.'

His arrogant statement infuriated her. She was disturbed by the electricity between them, and a host of sharp words raced through her mind. She restricted them to a stormy, 'And what do you base that opinion on, considering you hardly know me?'

'I know you better than you think,' he fired back.

'Is that a fact?' she snapped.

She turned away from him to continue with her unpacking, meaning for him to take her cue and leave the room. But, instead of obliging her, he caught hold of her wrist, spinning her back to face him.

'Yes, it is a fact,' he said, an edge of harshness in his voice. 'And the sweet, pliant person you become when you're simpering all over Marc isn't the real you.'

'I suppose you're an authority on my personality,' she flashed sarcastically.

'I ought to be. I've known you three years.'

'Then what is the real me?'

'A passionate witch with a temper to match her hair—on the rare occasions when she lets herself go,' he mocked, tilting her chin up.

Her eyes blazed as she realised that he had needled her into losing her cool with him. With an amused smile he released her and strode to the door, closing it behind him.

Her green silk nightgown was lying uppermost in the open suitcase on the bed. It was the closest thing to hand and she snatched it up, sorely tempted to throw it at the door to vent her pent-up vexation. She brought the impulse under control, wondering stormily why she was letting Jeb Hunter anger her so. The very fact that he was scathing about Marc was an endorsement of her fiancé's character. Taking a calming breath, she smoothed out the nightgown she was clutching, folded it, and put it away in a drawer.

She was still unpacking when a short while later her sister put her head round the door. 'Gwenyth, Dad wants you.'

'I'll be right down,' she answered.

Crossing the hall, she heard her father's voice. 'Come round for dinner on Monday as you can't manage tonight.'

'Thanks,' Jeb answered.

At least she wouldn't be forced to endure any more of his aggravating sarcasm on her first evening home, Gwenyth thought with relief as she went into the drawing-room. Her father glanced up.

'Jeb's just off,' he informed her, obviously assuming that she'd want to thank him before he went for meeting her at the airport.

Drawing on a long training in good manners, she said, her tone pleasant though her eyes were cool, 'I'll see you out.' She objected to being indebted to him, but forced herself to add, 'It was nice of you to pick us up.'

'And why do you suppose I did?' he asked as they crossed the hall.

She gave him a puzzled glance. 'What do you mean?'

'If you remember, you said I never did anything without an ulterior motive,' he mocked.

Her chin tilted to a defiant angle as they halted by the front door. 'Do you want me to take it back?' she asked.

Amusement glittered briefly in his hawkish blue eyes. 'From your point of view it was a fair assessment. But you forgot to add one thing when you were listing the reasons why you dislike me.'

'What was that?'

'I always get what I go after.'

There was something almost portentous about his arrogant assertion. Conscious of a strange, uneasy prickling at the back of her neck, she challenged, 'Is that a boast?'

'No, it's a statement of fact.' He opened the front door. 'I'll see you and lover boy tomorrow.'

Her hostile gaze followed him as he strode outside, the sunlight gleaming on his thick dark hair.

CHAPTER THREE

'IT'S A long time since I've been here,' Gwenyth commented to Marc as she slowed down for the entrance to the quarries the next morning.

The security guard posted at the gatehouse with its large glass windows peered to view the occupants of the Metro. Recognising Gwenyth, he indicated with a wave of his hand that she could drive on through.

They passed the notice giving the times of blasting for that day and then turned on to the curved road, banked with wild rhododendron bushes, which led towards the Brynteg Mining Company's offices. It ran along the rim of one of the open-cast quarries where mechanical diggers, insignificant in the massive excavation, were loading up the lorries. The slate would then be transported to the mill for cutting into blocks.

Despite the reclamation work that had gone on, tips of slate seemed to be everywhere, creating a harsh landscape in barren contrast to the surrounding slopes with their covering of bracken, heather and ranks of conifers. Against the quarry face, men in navy blue reefer jackets moved about, their yellow safety helmets showing up brightly. Every now and then a heavily laden truck trundled past them, raising dust in its wake.

When they arrived at the mine office, Gwenyth was pleased to learn from his secretary that Jeb was likely to be in a meeting all morning. He had evidently made a number of staff changes since her father had been in charge, and it was the first time she had met Lawrence Jones, the lean and dynamic personnel manager who showed them round.

He started their tour by taking them back down to reception, the décor of which reflected the company's image of progress coupled with success. The large floor area was plushly carpeted in grey and red. Chrome and red leather armchairs were grouped around a teak coffee table. Spanning the far wall was a magnificent mural in the shape of three open fans, made entirely from slate. Lawrence led them towards it.

'This mural demonstrates the skill of our craftsmen,' he began. 'Each piece has been cut by fretsaw out of bundles of wafer-thin slices of slate. The reason slate makes such excellent roofing material is because it can be split thinly and yet is very robust.'

Marc examined the mural closely, obviously impressed by it. 'I'd no idea slate came in this variety of colours,' he commented.

'At Brynteg the slates are blue-grey, but to get a more artistic effect they've been mixed here with the reds and greens of Bethesda.'

Having talked about the mining techniques necessary to work the five slate beds at Brynteg, the personnel manager showed them over the mill. Although Gwenyth had watched the quarrymen at work before, she still found it fascinating to see how, with a smart tap of a hammer on a chisel, they split off the thin layers from the squared-off slabs of blue-grey slate.

It was all so interesting that the time went quickly.

They had looked round the power house and were outside again when Lawrence said to Marc, 'Most of the mine's worked in the open, but I expect you'd like a look underground while you're here.'

'That would be interesting,' he agreed. As if joking he added, 'I take it that it's perfectly safe. I saw the notice warning of blasting when we drove in.'

'Yes, it's completely safe,' Lawrence assured him. 'That notice refers to the open-cast mines. Underground, the only time there's blasting is when a new chamber is being opened up. In any case, we'll only be going down to level one.'

Pushing back her silken cascade of bright hair that was blowing in the breeze, Gwenyth said, 'I'll meet you back in Reception, then, Marc.'

'You don't want to come?' Marc seemed surprised.

She glanced at the personnel manager with a smile. 'Despite a new boss, I don't suppose the old rule's changed?' she asked.

'You're right.' He smiled back. 'It hasn't.'

'What rule is this?' Marc asked, puzzled by the exchange.

'Women aren't allowed below the surface because it's thought to be unlucky.' Gwenyth explained the long-standing tradition at Brynteg.

'You mean Mr Hunter's superstitious?' There was amusement coupled with a slight jeer in Marc's voice.

'Privately, I very much doubt it,' Lawrence answered, 'but he's a good manager and he's got more sense than to get on the wrong side of his work-force for no reason.'

Gwenyth had little doubt that Lawrence was right. Jeb's decision to uphold the tradition would be based on shrewd management, not superstition. He had

not been welcomed when he had taken over at
Brynteg three years ago. The men were Welsh-
speaking, with strong bonds of kinship, families
having worked together at the mine for generations.
Her father had been one of them, and when Jeb had
superseded him, for the first time in the mine's long
history they had been subjected to the authority of
an outsider. It had caused considerable resentment,
yet ironically the nickname of *yr estron*, the foreigner,
had since come to be a title of respect. Increased
productivity under Jeb's management had brought
larger pay-packets and, with the quarry's expansion,
there had been more scope for promotion. She
doubted that Jeb cared that he still wasn't universally
liked. What counted was that he had the esteem and
loyalty of his work-force.

Back in Reception she took a seat, and was leafing
through a company magazine when the swing-doors
to her right opened. She glanced up to see Jeb come
in, strikingly male in a white shirt and grey suit that
accentuated the honed strength of his build. His
chiselled features didn't appeal to her, but she had to
admit, despite herself, that for women who liked
those types of looks he was arrestingly attractive.

A faint prickling stirred at the back of her neck as
their eyes met and he strode in her direction. Somehow even his walk seemed to antagonise her. It was
so very much that of a man used to coming on the
scene to take charge and produce results.

Surprised to see him, she began, bristling a little as
she always did with him, 'Your secretary said you
were going to be in a meeting all morning.'

His mouth quirked in a knowing smile. As though

he read her thoughts, he mocked, 'Were you hoping to avoid me?'

'Of course not,' she denied. She had briefly lost her temper with him yesterday, but this morning she was determined to revert to being cool, polite and distant. She had learned from her clash with him in her bedroom that sparks between them only created more sparks. 'Why should I want to avoid you?'

She was wearing a sleeveless white top that showed off her light honey-gold tan and a full, brightly patterned skirt. Green sandals, which matched her long beads and the splashes of colour in her skirt, showed off slim, chorus-line legs.

Jeb's gaze, frankly masculine and assessing, swept over her. It lingered briefly on her crossed legs and, instinctively, she adjusted the hem of her skirt so that it covered her knee. Amusement flickered in his blue eyes, and made her own spark in return. He had looked at her that way deliberately to unsettle her and she hadn't disappointed him.

'In which case come through to my office and I'll get my secretary to make some coffee,' he said.

She was reluctant to spend any time at all with him, but couldn't think how to decline his offer without showing him that her act of cool indifference was a sham. 'Are you sure you can spare the time?' she asked.

'I make time for the things that are important. By the way, how's your father this morning?'

'Dad's fine,' she answered.

Jeb was the last person she would confide in that she was a shade concerned about her father. She didn't know if gashing his leg had depressed him, but beneath the cheerful façade he seemed vaguely troubled.

With a couple of quick steps, she attempted unsuccessfully to avoid the proprietorial touch of Jeb's hand against her back as he escorted her across the reception area. It required a strong effort of will not to push it away.

His secretary looked up from her typewriter as they went into his outer office. In her early thirties, she had smooth ivory skin, dark hair and a brisk, competent manner. Gwenyth didn't doubt that, to be working for Jeb, she was every bit as efficient as she looked. Without knowing why she was interested, she checked to see if the woman wore a wedding ring. She did.

'Styne and Co have been on the phone this morning,' she informed Jeb. 'They'd like their order brought forward to the beginning of next month if possible. I've left the message on your desk.'

'I'll get back to them.' His voice was resolute and businesslike. It occurred to Gwenyth that she had never heard him raise it. He didn't need to in order to get things done. 'Meanwhile, Delyth, we'd like coffee.'

'Of course.' With a deferential smile, his secretary acknowledged his request.

Jeb guided Gwenyth into his office and closed the door behind them. She wasn't claustrophobic, and she could have gone into the narrowest, deepest tunnel on level five of the mine without a qualm. But here, alone with Jeb Hunter, even though the office was spacious, she was aware of a curious sense of unease.

'Make yourself comfortable,' he invited.

As he spoke he moved away from her. She wondered if she had imagined the touch of irony in his voice. Breathing more easily, she glanced around his office.

It was very much as she would have expected. A personal computer stood on his L-shaped desk, which indicated a heavy but well-organised workload. A black leather chair was placed behind it, while two others, obviously meant for visitors, stood in front. His office was austerely masculine, reflecting the tastes of a pragmatist who also had an appreciation of what was aesthetically pleasing.

Large windows gave a spectacular view of the road in. On either side of it were the open-cast workings with the mountains behind forming a sweeping backdrop. Picture-sized black and white photographs of the quarry as it had looked in the 1890s adorned the walls, providing a link with the past while serving as a reminder of the benefits of modern technology.

A leather sofa curved to fit one of the angles of the room. Together with a low onyx coffee-table, it provided a setting for less formal discussions. On a large table near the door was a model of the quarry showing all the current developments.

Glad of a distraction, she walked over to look at it. Constructed to scale it gave a bird's-eye view of the whole site, showing the offices, roads, narrow-gauge railway and open-cast quarries. Looking at it, she thought that Jeb didn't need a model to grasp the complexity of the business. He could look down mentally on the whole complex, master of all he surveyed. It galled her a little to have to acknowledge his business acumen.

'This is the first time you've been here since your father sold up, isn't it?' he commented.

'Why would I visit the quarries after you'd taken over?'

'Is it Morgan pride, or loyalty to your father that means you can't accept me as the new owner?' he asked, a mocking quirk to his mouth.

'It's neither,' she informed him with thinly veiled hostility. 'It's just that I think the place was run better when Dad was in charge.'

'For the first time since 1904 the quarry has an expanding labour force again,' he stated in reply. 'Philanthropic management and the drive for increased profitability don't have to conflict.'

Rather than concede that he had a point, she said with light sarcasm, 'I'm sure you're very philanthropic.'

'Successful men scare you, don't they?' he remarked lazily. 'I imagine that's why you've picked up with Marc.'

'Marc *is* a success,' she contradicted him promptly.

'Or does nepotism make it seem that way?'

'Marc may come from a rich and influential family, but he's got on through his own merits,' she flared tartly, before warning, 'If your aim is to start a quarrel, Jeb, I'm not going to oblige you. But I'll tell you one thing: there's no way I'd ever get in tow with a man like you! You may be successful, but you're also aggressive and ruthless!'

Her fiery observation obviously amused him, and she realised that, within only minutes of making the resolution not to lose her temper with him, she had broken it. Annoyed, she turned back to the model and commented, 'You've made a lot of changes.'

'And you don't like that, do you?' he said sardonically, coming to stand beside her.

She hoped he didn't notice that she tensed slightly. It wasn't change she disliked as much as her awareness of his advantage over her in height, and the way he reminded her of a beautifully aligned but predatory animal.

Without lifting her gaze from the model, she told him, 'I'm not against progress. Neither was my father.' Under the pretence of studying the developments shown in the far corner of the model she put a safer distance between them, and asked, 'What's happening here?'

'That's more reclamation work that's going on. I intend developing the whole area as a tourist attraction. It will involve some half a million pounds of investment, but the idea is to open a half-mile level section of the slate mines to the public.'

Impressed by the scheme, she glanced up and enquired, 'Who'll be in charge of that?'

'I haven't decided yet, but I'll want someone with a good background in public relations.'

As he was speaking, his secretary came in with the coffee. Leaving it on his desk, she went out as unobtrusively as she had entered.

'I believe you wear the same perfume as Delyth,' Jeb noted as he walked over to the desk.

'Givenchy III happens to be a favourite of mine,' she answered.

He laughed softly, a rich, masculine sound. 'You've changed since you've been away. Before, you wouldn't have chosen such a sophisticated and evocative fragrance.'

Both the sensual note to his voice and his personal

observation unsettled her. She was careful to avoid
the accidental brush of his fingers as he handed her
coffee-cup to her.

'It must be Marc's influence,' she replied.

'I'd be surprised.' His voice became dry for an
instant. 'But, just the same, the perfume suits you.'

Feeling the need to put some space between them,
she took her coffee-cup with her and walked over to
the window. She was wishing she had said that she'd
wait for Marc in the car. For some reason there was
too much static in the air, just as there had been
yesterday when she and Jeb had been alone. She
couldn't analyse it, but instinctively she knew it was
threatening.

She took a sip of the scalding liquid, determined to
appear at ease however much her nerves were tensed
with an awareness of some intangible danger. Coolly
she said, 'Don't flirt with me, Jeb. I'm not interested.'

He perched lazily on the desk, a big, powerful
man, yet graceful with it. The grey material of his
trousers outlined the firm muscles of his long thighs.
More than ever it seemed necessary to feign an
interest in the heavily laden lorries that were making
their way towards the exit of the quarry.

'Why should it bother you that I find you attractive?' he asked, a caressing inflexion to his charismatic voice.

Her startled gaze swung to him. There was a
roguish glint in his blue eyes as he observed her, and
she felt a sense of relief. In that instant, when she
had thought he was serious, her heart had been
beating much too fast.

'You find that hard to believe?' he went on.

'Impossible,' she said firmly. 'We've never even liked each other.'

As she spoke she set her coffee-cup down on the window-sill. She felt too on edge to drink.

'No, to date our track record hasn't been too good,' he agreed.

She found his tone hard to interpret, but instinct told her that he was making fun of her. He had called her sophisticated a moment ago. She wished it were true. Then she would know how to deal with a man like Jeb Hunter in a better way than hiding behind a chilly façade. It would be satisfying to be able to fight him on his own terms.

He strolled round behind his desk, opening a drawer to take out a gift-wrapped packet that was tied with a gold bow, the ends of which curled attractively.

'As I wasn't sure if you were having an engagement party, I thought I'd give you this now,' he said.

She felt wrong-footed. It was hard to accept an engagement present from him when a moment ago they'd been fencing. Managing as best she could to appear gracious, she moved to accept it.

'How kind of you,' she said. 'But really, you shouldn't have bothered. What is it?'

'Open it and see.'

She sat down and undid the pretty gift-wrapping to find a long, slim box that was embossed with the name of the craft shop it had come from. She lifted the lid, expecting to find that he had chosen some impersonal object for her new home. Anger blazed in her cheeks as she saw how very wrong she had been. Far from an impersonal gift, he had presented

her with a love spoon, a custom long associated in
Wales with courtship.

Any idea that she was mistaken was speedily
dispelled as she read the carved initials entwined on
the intricate sycamore handle with its worked vines,
bay leaves and small, decorative spheres. He had
even chosen a spoon with twin bowls.

The phone on his desk rang, but she was much too
angry to take any notice of his brief reply to the
message his secretary gave him. Her amber eyes
sparkled with the force of her outrage. He replaced
the receiver and, as he did so, she surged to her feet.
With her bright hair swinging round her shoulders
in a fiery halo, she slapped the box down on his desk
and began, 'If this is your idea of a joke, I don't think
it's the least bit funny!'

There was a satisfied quirk to his masculine mouth.
With the same purposefulness that was in his face,
he walked round his desk to her, virile, rugged and
very much in control of her explosion of anger, the
fuse of which he had deliberately lit.

'I thought the significance of a Welsh love spoon
wouldn't be lost on you,' he observed tauntingly.

It certainly wasn't. She was only too well aware
that such spoons were a token of amorous pursuit.
Trembling with fury that he dared be so bold, she
demanded, 'Are you making a pass at me?'

He gave a soft, diabolical chuckle. 'Is that a blush
of temper in your cheeks, or excitement?' he
enquired.

'I've no desire to be one of your women, Jeb
Hunter!' she flashed.

She wished she had the nerve to slap his swarthy
face, but it wasn't only her upbringing which stopped

her. It was the vague comprehension that to do so in such a highly charged atmosphere of sexual tension would be asking for trouble.

'Haven't you?' he jibed. 'University hasn't taught you much about yourself, has it?'

In an upsurge of panic she shied away from him. His very masculinity seemed to be a threat to her, making her breathing quicken.

'It's taught me to recognise a wolf when I see one!' she shot back.

To madden her still further, he appeared to think that she was referring to her fiancé. Amusement glittered in his blue eyes. 'I wouldn't call Marc a wolf, exactly. He's more a sheep in wolf's clothing.' Cleverly, Jeb had turned the usual idiom around.

Because she was angry, it took her a moment to grasp his meaning. When she did her temper flared anew. 'Don't you dare insult my fiancé!' she blazed. 'He's more of a man than you are any day!'

'What about any night?' Jeb drawled. 'Or aren't you sleeping with him yet?'

She breathed in sharply, his intimate question catching her off balance. 'That's none of your business!' she reminded him shortly.

'I want you myself,' he told her, putting into words what his gift had already implied. 'That makes me curious.'

'Then you can go on being curious!' she said stormily.

His blue gaze took in the rapid rise and fall of her small breasts and the colour in her cheeks. When she was cool and composed she was strikingly attractive, but angry she was a firebrand of beauty.

'I don't have to be,' he said with an easy smile.
'You've already given me the answer I wanted.'

'You're even more hateful than I thought!' she
exploded.

'Does Marc have any idea what a temper you've
got?' he demanded, a glint of satisfaction in his eyes.

'With Marc I don't have a temper!'

'Then he obviously doesn't arouse you the way I
do,' he answered.

Her fingers itched with the temptation to hit him,
but with a fierce effort of will she succeeded in
containing her anger. To slap him would merely
demonstrate the validity of his observation. Curling
her fingers tightly into her palms, she snapped,
'Rather than listen to any more comments from you,
I'd prefer to wait for my fiancé in Reception.'

'You won't have to wait,' Jeb informed her. 'He's
already down there.' He pressed the intercom on his
desk. 'Delyth, show Mr Brassac to my office, would
you?'

For an instant Gwenyth stared at him in disbelief.
Then she faltered, 'You mean. . .You mean he's been
waiting in Reception all this time?' Her voice
strengthened as she made the accusation.

'Only the last couple of minutes. Delyth notified
me of his arrival while you were unwrapping your
present. You were too absorbed to notice.'

Her eyes blazed murderously at his mocking comment. Seething with her inability to express even one
fraction of her fury, she turned and marched towards
the door. It was the command in Jeb's voice which
compelled her to stop.

'Before you leave,' he said. 'I want to have a word
with your fiancé. You might as well be present.'

She spun back to face him. 'To tell him what?' she challenged. 'That you've had the gall to make a pass at me?' The sarcasm in her voice was replaced with vehemence. 'I wish you would. I'd love to see him hit you.'

Jeb sat down behind his desk and nonchalantly picked up the telephone message which Delyth had put there earlier. Reading it, he asked, without looking up. 'You mean *he* might have the nerve, although you didn't?'

Her lips parted slightly and then closed again. So he had noticed her tightly clenched hands! Damn the man, did nothing ever escape his hawkish perception?

The fact that, when she was simmering with the force of the emotions he had aroused in her, he could be calmly continuing with his work only increased the storm that was raging inside her. Glaring at him with eyes that were twin amber flames, she promised, 'One day I swear I'll find the nerve!'

He glanced up. 'I'll look forward to it,' he answered with an amused lift of his dark brows.

It seemed typical that Marc's entrance at that moment should give Jeb the victory of having the last word. She checked the reply she would otherwise have flashed back with. The interruption made her realise how close she'd been to flaring up with him again. Why was it that lately she rose to every hateful comment he made? Everything he said seemed to bring out in her the need to fight him.

'I hope you found the tour of the quarry interesting, Marc,' he began, his manner faintly derisive despite the semblance of politeness.

'Very,' Marc agreed. It was apparent from his tone that beneath the surface *bonhomie* he no more took to Jeb than Jeb took to him. 'I'm only sorry to have kept Gwenyth waiting. I see you have kept her company.'

He was obviously about to suggest that they leave when his gaze fell on the gift box and wrapping paper on Jeb's desk. He picked it up, his voice slightly more amiable as he said, 'What's this? An engagement present?'

His questions precipitated what Jeb had clearly intended saying all along. 'Far from it,' he answered, his eyes glinting with malicious humour. 'It's what you might call a challenge.'

'A challenge?' Marc repeated with a puzzled frown.

'It's a love spoon,' Gwenyth explained, anger taking over as she recovered from her initial disbelief at Jeb's statement. 'It means. . .'

She faltered, finding it impossible to express in words what it did mean. Jeb's mouth twitched sardonically.

'It means what?' Marc demanded.

Since she was under no illusions as to what kind of man Jeb was, she knew perfectly what his intentions were. To say that the gift meant that he intended paying court to her was to use a phrase that was euphemistic. What he had said was that he wanted her. It was as basic as that, and there was no other way of saying it.

Taking a deep breath, she stated, feeling herself blush with a mixture of indignation and embarrassment, 'It means that he wants me.'

'I thought it only fair to give you warning, Marc,' Jeb drawled in confirmation of what she had said. 'I don't regard your engagement to Gwenyth as binding. So, as of now, you have a competitor.'

Marc evidently couldn't believe he'd heard correctly. His gaze swung to Gwenyth. '*Comment*?' he demanded, as though needing her to translate Jeb's challenge into French for him to be able to credit it. '*Ce n'est pas possible!*'

A quiver of unease ran down her spine. Instinctively she took a quick step forward. The angry incredulity in Marc's voice made her certain that if she didn't intervene promptly the two men would come to blows.

But her action was unnecessary. Marc, who had stiffened at Jeb's arrogant announcement, remained standing stock-still, glaring at his opponent. A nerve jumped in his jaw as his fingers tightened on the love spoon. 'If this is your challenge,' he said, after a seething pause, 'then I accept it. But you won't win!'

Jeb smiled faintly. He picked up his phone, pressing out the number he wanted. Obviously he didn't think Marc's prediction was worth a flat contradiction. Instead he jibed lightly, a steely light in his blue eyes, 'Don't you know the English expression, faint heart never won fair lady?' Receiving an answer from the number he had dialled, he went on, 'Tony Styne? Jeb Hunter here. I'm returning your call.'

Marc's mouth tightened angrily. Taking Gwenyth's arm he opened the door for her. 'Come on, *chérie*,' he said tersely. 'Let's go.'

CHAPTER FOUR

NEITHER of them spoke until they were out of the building. His hand at Gwenyth's elbow, Marc glanced back in the direction of Jeb's office as they crossed the car park.

'The incredible nerve of that man!' he exclaimed with muted force. 'He deserved to have his spoon pushed down his throat, along with his arrogant words.' They reached the car and, as he opened the driver's door for her, he added, 'What's more, it was no idle challenge.'

Still simmering with indignation, Gwenyth was equally certain that it wasn't. Though the sun was warm on her arms, a strange prickling seemed suddenly to trace over her skin, as though something brushed her lightly in warning.

'Jeb can issue as many challenges as he likes,' she said emphatically, 'but it won't get him anywhere.'

'Are you cold?' Marc asked.

Refusing to admit, even to herself, the cause of the little shiver that had gone through her, she shook her head. 'I'm fine,' she insisted. 'Anyway, my cardigan's on the back seat.'

She got into the Metro while Marc walked round to duck in beside her. He put the love spoon on the dashboard and said with a short laugh, 'Imagine! I thought he'd given us an engagement present!'

'When he handed me the box I made the same mistake,' she said. She jabbed the key into the ignition and then sat back, too ruffled to want to start the car immediately. 'I just can't get over his monstrous conceit!' she exclaimed. 'That he could even *think* I'm interested in him!'

'It's obvious that not many women have turned him down, or he wouldn't be so cocksure of himself.'

'Well, his arrogant charisma's never had the slightest appeal for me!'

'Which is why he wants you.' Marc frowned.

'What do you mean?'

'It's because you've never fallen for him that he wants you,' Marc explained. 'I get the impression that to Jeb Hunter any obstacle is a challenge.'

'I suppose that's why he's such a success in business,' she said, hating him.

Yesterday he had somehow dominated her homecoming, but she wasn't going to let him tarnish today as well. About to make a suggestion, she turned her head to glance at her fiancé. Dark, handsome and suave, he was everything she could want in a husband. The stormy light faded from her eyes.

Why ever, she wondered, was she letting herself get so worked up about Jeb? Generally her anger was quickly spent. It was ridiculous to be sitting here, upset and fuming, when no matter what Jeb said or did she would always belong to Marc.

'Let's forget about the love spoon,' she announced. 'We've only got a few days together before you fly back to France. I don't want Jeb to spoil them.'

'You're right,' Marc agreed.

Reaching out his hand, he traced the line of her neck beneath her hair before drawing her into his arms. She went willingly, closing her eyes to savour the feel of his lips. When finally he lifted his mouth from hers, he still stayed close, pressing tiny kisses against her cheek.

'A Metro's a bit small for this sort of thing,' he murmured. 'Not to mention the fact that we're in full view of the mine offices.'

Slightly shy about kissing in public, she laughed at his teasing, but coloured a little as well. Exchanging a quick last kiss with him, she started the ignition. She pulled out of the parking space, her gaze sweeping the window of Jeb's office. There was no sign of him. She had known deep down that there wouldn't be. Yet with a slight twinge of guilt she knew, too, that partly why she had returned Marc's kiss so ardently was the hope that Jeb was witnessing it.

Banishing the man from her thoughts, she said with a smile, 'I don't know about you, but I'm ready for lunch.'

'Good idea,' Marc agreed. He was silent for a while, and then said with a frown, 'You realise that, since Jeb's a friend of your family's, he can call round almost any evening he chooses on some pretext or other to see you?'

She had suggested that they forget about Jeb, but he had come back into the conversation almost immediately.

'He'll get short shrift from me if he does,' she stated. 'The way I intend to freeze him from now on will make the Arctic seem positively warm by comparison.'

'That should deflate his ego nicely.' Marc laughed.

It was an infectious sound, making her laugh too. Suddenly she no longer felt furious about Jeb's declaration that he wanted her. Instead she was amused. With Marc's solitaire on her finger she was perfectly safe from Jeb. A malevolent sparkle came into her amber eyes as she thought of the immense satisfaction it was going to give her to put him in his place the next time she saw him.

She slowed down for the quarry gates and then drew to a halt as, to her surprise, the security guard came out of the gate-house and put up his hand for her to stop. She wound down her window.

'What is it, Lloyd?' she asked as the man walked over to speak to her. It was ridiculous, but her first assumption was that Jeb was ordering her and Marc back to his office.

Bending to her window, Lloyd said, 'Your father has been trying to contact you. He needs to speak to you urgently.'

'Whatever can have happened?' She voiced the anxious thought aloud.

'I don't think it's anything to worry about,' Lloyd reassured her quickly. 'If it had been, Mr Hunter would have said.'

'Jeb?'

'You'd already left the mine offices when your father phoned,' Lloyd explained. 'Mr Hunter called me on the off chance that I'd be able to stop you at the gate.'

'I see.' The smile she gave the security guard momentarily chased away her look of puzzlement. 'Thanks, Lloyd.'

Since they were only ten minutes from home, it was no trouble to drive back. Her mother was in the garden snipping off some rose blooms when they pulled up outside the house.

'It doesn't look as if there's been any great calamity in our absence,' Marc teased.

'No, but it must be something important or Dad would have let it wait,' she answered.

Catrin walked towards them as they got out of the car. 'Jeb managed to give you the message, then. He said he'd try to catch you,' she said, and then went on, 'Your bank's been on the phone, Marc. They'd like you to ring back as soon as possible.'

'I wonder why,' Marc answered. 'I'd better find out what the problem is.'

'The study's empty if you'd like to phone in there,' Catrin offered.

'Thank you.'

Gwenyth stayed in the garden chatting to her mother while Marc made the phone call. It was some time before he joined them again, his face set in serious lines.

'What's wrong, Marc?' she asked in concern.

'There's been an armed robbery at the bank. It happened in the early hours of this morning.'

'How awful!' Catrin exclaimed.

'Was anyone hurt?' Gwenyth asked.

'No, fortunately, but close on a quarter of a million has been stolen, without reckoning on what's been lost in the safe deposit boxes. That's why the bank's got on to me. I'll have to contact the owners, as well as deal with our insurers.'

'You mean you've got to go back?' Gwenyth queried.

'I'm afraid so,' he confirmed, looking suitably grave. 'I've phoned the airport. I can get a flight this evening.'

'Oh, Marc,' she said disappointedly. 'Isn't there anyone else who can handle it?'

'Not as efficiently as I can.' He squeezed her hand. 'I'm sorry too, but it can't be helped.'

She nodded. Making the best of it, she said, managing a small smile, 'I'll come with you to——'

'No, no,' Marc interrupted, a slight shading of self-importance in his tone. 'Much as I like the idea, there's no sense in your coming with me. I shan't have a minute's free time over the next few days.'

Gwenyth tried not to let his rejection of her make her feel nettled. Telling herself that he didn't mean to sound pompous, she said, 'I know that. I was going to suggest I drive you to the airport. What time do you have to be there?'

His flight was at nine-fifteen. She waited with him in the busy departure lounge until the announcement came over the tannoy. She gave him a last tiny wave as he went through the boarding gate and then, her hands in the pockets of her jacket, she walked slowly back the way she had come. Was it only yesterday that they had arrived together and she had felt so happy?

The thought brought Jeb into her mind. She flicked a bright strand of hair over her shoulder, and her heels tapped more smartly. She doubted it would take long before he found out that Marc had returned to France, but if he imagined for one instant that it left the field wide open for him, he'd soon discover how wrong he was.

The following morning a phone call from her fiancé lifted her spirits.

'You look happy,' Sian commented.

'I am. Marc's just rung me. The bank's promised to make his holiday up to him and he hopes to be back next Saturday,' Gwenyth answered, adding, 'I hoped he'd give me a call. That's why I stayed in.'

'Then how about driving to the coast this afternoon?' Sian suggested.

The tourist season had only just started, so that although the weather was beautiful they had the beach, which was a mixture of wave-smoothed pebbles and golden sand, almost to themselves. The mountains were serene in the sunlight, curving round the bay so that in the distance they seemed to rise up from the shimmering sea like a hazy blue peninsula.

Gwenyth slipped out of her sarong-style skirt, which matched her black and white bikini, oiled herself well and then sat down, looping her arms around her knees. Her gaze followed Ricky, who was down by the water's edge chasing the white wavelets which broke ceaselessly on the shore.

'This is the life,' Sian murmured as, having stripped off, she flopped down on the sand.

'Isn't it just?' Gwenyth agreed. With a contented sigh she lay back, too, and closed her eyes. The conversation gradually became spasmodic, and then finally lapsed altogether.

Drowsily Gwenyth listened to the keening cries of the gulls, enjoying the sun's caress on her bare skin. The call of the sea seemed to grow fainter. As her thoughts began to drift, Jeb came unbidden into her mind.

It was with a start that some while later she opened her eyes. 'What. . .what did you say?' she faltered, certain that her sister had spoken to her.

'Nothing,' Sian murmured with a smile. 'You've been asleep.'

She couldn't deny it. In fact, as her thoughts cleared and the recollection of what she had been dreaming flashed into prominence, she couldn't even attempt an answer. Shocked and ashamed of herself, she turned on to her stomach, resting her face on her arms so that her flaming cheeks were hidden.

In her dream she had been alone with Jeb in his office. They had been sitting on his black leather sofa when he had very gently grazed her cheek with his thumb. Her heart had jolted, an intense pleasurable shock going through her.

Tension had vibrated between them—dangerous, yet exciting. Still without speaking, Jeb had cupped her face with his hand, his fingers caressing her skin as, for a moment suspended in time, his eyes had searched hers. She'd looked up into their vivid blueness, the mesmerising spell unbroken even when his gaze had shifted to her lips. Her heart had been pounding with heavy beats as he'd bent his head. . .

Determined not to remember any more she sat up quickly. Shading her eyes against the brightness of the sun that glanced up off the sea, she announced, 'The tide's just right for a swim. Are you coming?'

Sian shook her head. 'I can't be bothered,' she said drowsily, letting a handful of sand trickle through her fingers.

'Lazy,' Gwenyth teased, striving hard to sound like her usual self.

She got to her feet and walked with lithe grace over the soft sand. The sea air tasted salty on her lips and she tossed her head as the breeze blew a strand of burnished hair across her face. As she neared the sea she broke into a run. She hated Jeb. How could she possibly have dreamed that he was kissing her and, worse, that she was enjoying it?

She splashed into the water and then waded deeper, catching her breath as she felt the chill of the salt water against her midriff. A larger wave surged towards her and, shivering a little, she plunged into it. Preferring not to go too far out of her depth, she swam parallel to the shore for some way. Then she turned on her back, letting the waves buffet her gently as she floated, gazing up through wet lashes at a dazzling sky.

Rationalising, she told herself that her dream was nothing more than a quirk of her subconscious. It was silly to give it any more thought. Turning again, she broke into a fast crawl. At last she waded shorewards and started back up the beach. A shade breathless from the exercise and the invigorating chill of the water, she dropped down beside Sian and reached for a towel.

'You should have come in,' she said. 'It's not cold.'

'No?' Sian queried sceptically. 'It looked jolly cold when you first went in.'

'You soon get used to it,' Gwenyth laughed, twisting her silken hair over her shoulder so that the water ran out of it. 'Anyway, it's bracing.'

'I'll take your word for it. I prefer sunbathing,' Sian answered. She pulled her denim jacket towards her and began hunting in its pockets for her purse. 'Now that you're back from your swim, I'm going to get a cold drink. Do you want one?'

'Please. I'll have a Coke.'

'OK. Shan't be long.'

Ricky, who was lying nearby, stood up, shook himself and then trotted after her. With the dog at her heels, Sian clambered up the steep bank of pebbles to the sea wall, while Gwenyth picked up the Simenon detective novel Marc had lent her and began to read.

The call of the gulls and the distant surge of the sea added to the warm tranquillity. Absently she reached behind her neck and pulled the bow of her halter-neck bikini top undone, so that she wouldn't get strap-marks as she tanned.

She hadn't been reading long when the rattle of shifting pebbles made her glance up. Her heart gave a lurch as she saw Jeb coming on to the beach. Swiftly she averted her gaze hoping that, since he was some way off, he hadn't noticed her.

She fumbled urgently with the ties of her bikini top, her face becoming hot when her long hair tangled in the bow. She swept her hair aside and tied the bow more securely, her senses warning her that Jeb was heading straight in her direction.

Hiding her agitation, she quickly picked up her detective novel again. When she'd made the resolve to freeze Jeb with chilly disdain, she hadn't known he would catch her half naked on the beach. A moment ago she had been enjoying the luxury of the warm sun on her skin. Now she felt alarmingly vulnerable in her black and white bikini, which suddenly seemed much too brief.

Determined to feign cool surprise at seeing him, she looked up slowly as his tall shadow fell across her, only to find that her heart was clamouring. It was a long while since she had seen him in casual clothes, and the impact of his raw virility as he towered above her made her feel practically breathless for an instant or two.

He was wearing a cream sweatshirt with a sports club emblem on the front, and blue jeans that showed strong, muscular thighs. In them he looked every bit as hard and fit as an athlete. When he was dressed in a grey business suit she found his masculinity disturbing, but at least it was tempered with urbanity. Now he looked ruggedly male, his virility somehow an active threat to her.

Forgetting that she had planned to crush him with icy aloofness she began, sounding every bit as defensive as she felt, 'What are you doing here, Jeb?'

'Admiring the view,' he drawled, sliding his hands into the pockets of his jeans as he dropped to his haunches beside her.

Instinctively her hand went to check that the bra of her bikini was securely in place. Amusement came into the blue eyes which travelled over her, lingering appreciatively on her curves. With a marked increase in both colour and coldness she said, 'Then may I suggest you admire the view somewhere else?'

Jeb ignored her request. 'What are you reading?' he asked, as he pulled his sweatshirt over his head.

She found she was staring at his naked chest with its matting of dark, curling hair. She saw that the muscles of his broad shoulders were full and rounded, while those of his stomach were flat and broad.

'*Maigret Hésite*,' she breathed in reply.

Hastily recollecting herself she returned her attention to her book, furious to find that for some reason her hand trembled slightly as she turned the page.

'I unsettle you, don't I?' Jeb remarked lazily.

She was antagonised by his blatant maleness, and his taunt was too much for her. She slapped the paperback face down on the sand. 'You don't unsettle me at all,' she contradicted him, her eyes sparkling dangerously. 'But after yesterday I simply don't have anything to say to you. Now, if you don't mind, I'd like to be left alone.'

'I thought you were enjoying my company,' Jeb mocked.

With great restraint she refrained from answering. Jeb stood up and, with a little stab of triumph, she thought she'd won. But he didn't move away and, puzzled, she glanced up to see that he was taking off his jeans. His broad back gleamed in the sunlight, navy swimming-trunks hugging his lean hips.

'Where's Marc today?' he enquired as he settled down beside her again. 'Has he abandoned you?'

Acutely aware of his nearness and of the dark hairs that curled on his strong upper thighs she said shortly, wondering how much longer she would succeed in keeping her temper, 'He's had to go back to France. There's been an armed robbery at his bank.'

'I suppose, like Maigret, he's solving the case single-handed,' Jeb jibed.

'I don't find that particularly funny,' she flared.

'I don't expect Marc would either, since he hasn't got much of a sense of humour.'

Not realising how stormy her amber eyes had become she demanded, 'Was he meant to take the love spoon you gave me as a joke?'

'No. I was perfectly serious about that,' he said, his gaze deliberately raking her.

She breathed in sharply. Her skin seemed to burn from the insolent caress of his blue eyes. 'Why do you persist in this?' she snapped.

'Why do *you* go on pretending?' he asked, quirking a sardonic brow at her.

'Pretending about what?' she demanded irritably.

'That you're not interested in going to bed with me.'

To her hot discomfort her memory chose that moment to remind her of the erotic dream she'd had about him. Scorched with a mixture of fury and shame, she couldn't even begin to think of a put-down. 'You. . .you leave me speechless!' she spluttered.

The masculine line of his mouth curved in an appreciative smile. 'You're very attractive when you're angry,' he observed.

She felt that she would explode with temper. 'You just listen to me,' she hissed. 'Despite your arrogant assumption, I'm not trembling with repressed desire for you. In fact, there's nothing on this earth that would ever induce me to share your bed!'

'Prove it, then,' he said softly. 'Kiss me.'

'Don't be so ridiculous!'

'Is it me you're scared of, or yourself?'

For an instant, uncertainty flickered in her eyes. The thought that he might have seen it made her insist contemptuously, 'I'm not afraid of you!'

'No?'

'No!' she flashed back.

He didn't answer, but his cynical smile told her how much weight her emphatic statement carried with him. She glared angrily at him, everything that was spirited in her rising to his infuriating challenge. Maybe, she reasoned, it would be no bad thing to establish that there had been no significance to her dream. She couldn't possibly be attracted physically to a man she despised, so what was the risk in kissing him?

Gathering her courage, she looked up at him with provocative defiance. 'I'm not afraid to kiss you,' she said, shifting her position so that she could link her fingers behind his neck.

Her gaze slipped to the firm but sensual line of his mouth. Her heart was suddenly thudding, but she couldn't draw back now. Bravado demanded that she continue with what she had begun. Her lashes fluttering down, she placed her lips lightly against his. Jeb's hands moved to her waist, holding her, yet making no attempt to pull her closer as she kissed each corner of his mouth.

Feeling as though she'd played with danger long enough, she let her hands fall from his neck. In a voice that was lightly scathing, if not quite as steady as she'd have liked, she murmured, 'Have I proved my point?'

'Now I'll prove mine.'

She saw the gleam in his eyes, but it was already too late. Before she could wedge a protesting hand between them, his mouth claimed hers. She made an angry noise in her throat as she tried to free herself. Jeb's kiss was hard and searching, his arms sliding further about her to hold her to the warmth of his strong, masculine body.

She dug her nails into his shoulders, trying to hurt him, but with no effect. His mouth continued to ravage hers. Unable to turn her head away, she felt as though she were drowning.

For an instant she stopped resisting and, in that moment, Jeb changed his kiss to one of deliberate seductiveness. A shiver of treacherous response went through her. Hit by vertigo, she tried to renew her efforts at fighting him, but Jeb was too quick to take advantage of the wayward fire that danced along her nerves. Her world seemed to spin as she felt his lips part hers.

Not knowing what she was doing, she tightened her hand round his neck. Jeb moved to hold her more intimately and she moaned a bewildered protest as she felt the warm sand against her back. Shocked at the fierce pagan pleasure he was arousing in her, she made a last, desperate effort to escape. His hard thigh moved across her own, thwarting her.

To her utter dismay she realised that she was losing, not to his superior strength, but to the urgent need he was stirring in her to respond. Her hands spread, clutching feverishly at the smooth warmth of his shoulders, as involuntarily she began to kiss him back, the movement of her lips complementing his. He cupped the swell of her breast, his thumb caressing her nipple.

The surge of pleasure made her gasp and, horrified at what she was allowing him to do, she broke free from him and scrambled to her feet. Her eyes blazed as she stared at him, her breasts rising and falling rapidly.

'I always knew you'd hold nothing back once you got started,' Jeb drawled as he too stood up, his breathing every bit as altered as her own. 'I don't know which turns me on more, your fiery temper, or that defiant frosty act you put on with me at times.'

Trembling with fury, she breathed, 'How dare you? How *dare* you kiss me like that? Don't you ever touch me again!'

'Why not?' he taunted. 'It's a little too late to tell

me you didn't like it. You made your pleasure very obvious.'

Her hand swung up to deny what he'd said, but, as always, Jeb's reactions were lightning-fast. He snatched hold of her wrist and, with her heart jolting, she realised that despite his apparent amusement an anger fiercer than her own lurked not far beneath the surface.

'Don't act too wild with me, Gwenyth, or I might be tempted to tame you,' he warned.

'You wouldn't know where to begin!'

'Wouldn't I?' he taunted softly, looking at the full curve of her mouth that still throbbed with the aftermath of his passion.

Intuition told her that to flash back with a defiant answer would be asking for him to kiss her again. Jeb's eyes glinted with humour as he saw from the furious sparks in her gaze the effort it cost her to master her temper. In a voice that bit with animosity, she said, 'In case you've forgotten, I happen to be engaged!'

'No, I haven't forgotten,' he answered, 'but for a moment or two just now you seemed to have forgotten completely. You'd do well to think about that.'

She snatched her wrist away from him. 'You're contemptible!' she snapped.

'Why don't you tell Marc about it,' he suggested sarcastically. 'It might galvanise him into action before I steal his girl in front of his eyes.'

She glared at him, before scooping up her belongings and stuffing them into her sister's beach bag. As though his statement didn't even merit a reply, she brushed past him. She marched up the beach, her lips compressed and her head held high. Yet mingled

with her anger was a stirring of apprehension. Jeb
had stated the other day that he always got what he
wanted. Just supposing he was right?

As she reached the top of the beach she saw Sian
coming towards her. Her sister climbed up on the
sea wall and then jumped down lightly from it on to
the pebbles.

'Hi,' she began, a shade breathlessly. 'Did I seem
gone a long time? I bumped into some friends in the
newsagent's and we got talking. Here's your Coke.'

'Thanks,' Gwenyth said.

Her amber eyes stormy, she glanced back down
the beach. Jeb was swimming out to sea, tanned
shoulders cleaving through the water in an effortless
crawl. His kiss had been so plundering and thorough
that she could still feel the pressure of his mouth on
hers. With a sharp little tug on the metal ring she
opened the can of Coke. Its coldness against her lips
as she took a sip of the iced drink erased the tingling
sensation.

'Let's go down to the sand again, where we were
sitting before,' Sian suggested.

'No!' The last thing she wanted was to encounter
Jeb again when he returned from his swim. She made
her answer sound less sharp by continuing, finding
it a struggle to conceal how thoroughly on edge she
was, 'I thought we'd drive to the next cove to make
a change of scene.'

'OK,' Sian agreed. She perched on the wall and
added with a smile, swinging her bare legs, 'Just as
long as you're not ready to go home yet.'

Gwenyth smiled back, determined to bring her
turbulent emotions under control.

'That's a jolly strong swimmer out in the bay,' her sister observed.

'It's Jeb,' Gwenyth told her shortly.

Sian shaded her eyes against the sun's brightness. 'So it is,' she agreed, waving vigorously. Far out at sea Jeb waved an answering hand. 'You know,' Sian commented, 'I think he fancies you.'

'Well, I can't stand him!'

'I'd rather like him as a brother-in-law,' Sian stated musingly.

'There's no chance of that! Anyway, what's wrong with Marc as a brother-in-law?'

'Nothing. He's very nice, but Jeb's good fun.'

'I find his sarcastic sense of humour infuriating,' Gwenyth muttered, wrapping her sarong-style skirt round her and slipping on her sandals.

She meant her reply to put an end to a disturbing subject, but instead her sister remarked chattily, 'He's going out with a real looker at the moment. She's from London, but she's brought Blaen Wern as a weekend cottage.'

Gwenyth wasn't the least bit interested in his love life, so it was in spite of herself that she asked, 'What makes her so striking?'

'She's got emerald-green eyes, and her dark hair's cut very short so that it focuses attention on them. Added to that, she's as slim as a pencil and she dresses in a way that's sporty but elegant.'

He really was totally without scruples, Gwenyth thought murderously. She'd always classed him as a womaniser, but the proof of it fanned her temper. To think he had dared to kiss her! But one thing was certain: he was never getting within kissing distance of her again.

CHAPTER FIVE

'You've changed your plans rather suddenly,' Catrin commented on Monday evening when Gwenyth announced that she was going out. 'I was so sure you'd be in, I'm making your favourite strawberry pavlova for dessert.'

'It looks mouth-watering.' Gwenyth smiled. 'Save me a piece and I'll have it tomorrow—that is, if Jeb doesn't eat half of it.'

Her mother, who was decorating the sides of the meringue shell with piped cream, glanced up. 'That's a bit uncalled for, isn't it?' she reproved mildly. 'Jeb always behaves in the most gentlemanly fashion.'

'Perhaps you don't know him as well as I do,' Gwenyth said darkly.

'Well, one thing's for sure, you two certainly aren't indifferent to each other.'

'What exactly do you mean by that?' Gwenyth demanded.

'I've noticed that lately the two of you can't seem to stop sparring with each other.'

'That's Jeb's fault,' Gwenyth defended herself. Seeing the thoughtful glance her mother gave her she asked, 'What are looking at me like that for?'

'I was wondering why Jeb makes you so angry.'

Gwenyth coloured slightly and stated, 'He's just plain infuriating.'

'Well, I find him good company.' Her mother

laughed. 'I'm hoping that, when he comes round for dinner tonight, he'll cheer Derec up a bit.'

The mutinous light in Gwenyth's eyes was replaced by concern. So she hadn't been imagining it when she'd felt that her father seemed preoccupied. 'Do you know what's bothering him?' she asked.

'I don't think it's anything specific, but he's smoking more than he does usually.'

'Maybe gashing his leg has depressed him.'

'That could be it,' Catrin agreed. 'But, whatever it is, he'd tell me if it was anything serious.'

Realising that what her mother had said was true, Gwenyth put the matter out of her mind. Her parents were so close that, if some problem was weighing on her father, her mother would know about it.

Devoted to each other, they shared a wonderful rapport, she thought. She hoped her own marriage would be equally strong. Immediately she was impatient with herself. Of course it would be. She loved Marc and he loved her. There would never be any gulf of misunderstanding between them.

Looking forward to their being together again, when Saturday came she was at the airport in good time to meet him. He was one of the first passengers to emerge off the flight into the large arrivals hall.

'Marc!' She laughed his name as she ran towards him to be wrapped tightly in his embrace. 'It's so good to see you!'

'It's good to be back,' he said warmly, kissing her.

When they finally drew apart she asked, her eyes shining happily, 'Did you get everything sorted out at the bank?'

'Yes, things are pretty much back to normal now.'

With her arm tucked affectionately through his, they walked towards the exit. Marc told her in detail about the robbery, and as he got into her car alongside her she asked, 'Do you think the police will catch the gang?'

'Apparently they're working on several promising leads,' he said. 'But let's forget about the bank. Right now we've got more important things to talk about.'

'Such as?' she teased.

'Such as, I've missed you,' he murmured softly.

'Me, too,' she whispered.

As she spoke he moved to claim her mouth with his. She slid her arms up around his neck, her eyes closing, meaning to savour a more intimate kiss now that they were alone in the car. Her sun-dress was backless and the buttons on Marc's sleeve pressed into her skin, but she didn't care. It felt too good to be in his arms again.

His lips parted hers and in that moment the recollection of Jeb's plundering kiss suddenly shook her. The memory was so vivid, sensual and disturbing, she pulled away from Marc in abrupt confusion. It was only as her dazed eyes met his that she realised what she had done.

'What's the matter?' Marc asked, a thread of puzzled laughter in his voice.

She looked away, unable to sustain his gaze. She couldn't explain her reaction even to herself, let alone to him. Seizing on an excuse for her behaviour, she said with a rueful smile, 'Your buttons were hurting me.'

Marc tilted her chin towards him and grazed her lips lightly with his. 'Sorry,' he murmured. Settling back in his seat he asked, 'How do you feel about going out to dinner tonight? Do you know anywhere we can hold hands across a candle-lit table?'

'How about romantic music as well as a candle-lit table?' she suggested, smiling.

'Sounds perfect,' Marc approved.

'Then I know the very place.'

The hotel she was thinking of was set high up in attractively landscaped grounds, which overlooked the road and the estuary beyond. Panoramic windows capitalised on a view of the river seen through fans of larch and conifer that was breathtaking at sunset.

Marc was even more approving of her choice when they entered the dining-room together. Pools of candle-light played on the pink and white table-cloths, while gentle music provided a pleasant background to the muted buzz of talk and laughter and the tinkle of glass and silver.

'It's no wonder I'm under your spell,' Marc murmured when they were seated at a table for two beside the dance-floor. 'You look lovelier than ever this evening.'

'Are you under my spell?' she asked with soft-voiced flirtatiousness.

'You know I am. I can't take my eyes off you. Green is certainly your colour.'

She was wearing a bias slip of a dress in jade silk. With ribbon-thin straps it showed off the graceful lines of her neck and shoulders, while her chestnut hair was braided into a French plait that was severe but elegant.

'Sometimes I wish I could wear pink or, better still, red,' she admitted.

'Red's a dangerous colour. It's used for warnings.'

'What's wrong with that?' she joked.

'You mean you like playing with danger?'

His teasing words made her remember her reck-lessness in responding to Jeb's dare that she kiss him to prove that there was no spark of attraction between them. With a forced smile she shook her head. She fully intended telling Marc how she had met Jeb on the beach, but to mention it now would be to break the mood.

She was laughing at one of his polished anecdotes, when some sixth sense made a faint prickling stir at the back of her neck. Like a fawn scenting danger, she glanced up instinctively, her laughter dying in her throat as she saw that Jeb had just walked into the dining-room.

His tall, lean figure was framed by the door behind him, the slim, dark-haired woman who was at his side barely reaching his shoulder. Gwenyth's pulse quickened, she thought with anger, as she stared across the space between them into his strikingly masculine face with its ruggedly chiselled features. Of all the luck that he should choose the very hotel that she and Marc had come to!

'What's wrong?' Marc asked.

Dragging her gaze away from the hawkish blue eyes of their mutual enemy, she said, 'Jeb's just walked in.'

Marc glanced over his shoulder. Jeb was being shown to one of the best tables in the dining-room by the head-waiter. His hand rested lightly against his partner's slim waist. Noting it, Marc turned back to Gwenyth.

'Jeb seems to have forgotten about his challenge

very quickly,' he observed. 'When he thought about it afterwards, he obviously realised he couldn't win.'

'I've never known Jeb to give up on anything he wants,' she answered, a shading of wariness in her voice.

'Then this will be a first for him,' Marc stated as he reached across the table to take her hand. His fingers enclosing hers, he asked, 'Now, when are we going to fix the date for our wedding?'

'What's wrong with fixing it right now?' She smiled, feeling safe once again. She was a fool to get Jeb's challenge out of proportion.

'You know my wishes,' Marc told her. 'I'd like us to be married this September.'

'I don't want us to have to be apart for a year either,' she agreed, 'but, Marc, I'm so close to finishing my course——'

'We've discussed this before, *chérie*,' he cut across her. 'You already speak French fluently. You don't need a degree in the subject to prove it.'

'No, but——'

'But what?' he pressed.

For an instant she was tempted to capitulate. After all, the sooner she was married to Marc, the sooner she would be beyond Jeb's reach. Immediately, she was cross with herself. Why should she let a man she despised and hated influence her decision? She wasn't afraid of Jeb Hunter. She had Marc's love to protect her and, whether they married this coming September or the following June, Jeb would never come between them.

'Let me talk to Dad about giving up my course, first,' she said.

'Darling, you're twenty-one! Surely you can make your own decisions without consulting your father?'

'Of course I can,' she asserted. 'But Dad's paid for me to go to university for three years. I don't want to disappoint him and, apart from that, getting my degree matters to me, too.'

'Don't *I* matter to you?' Marc asked.

'You know you do,' she protested, adding in appeal, 'Please, Marc, don't pressurise me. June's only nine months on from September.'

Marc sighed and released her hand. 'All right. Tell your father that you want to give up your course and then we'll talk about the date for our wedding again.'

She looked at him, realising that he hadn't listened to her at all. Before he'd embarked on his banking career, Marc had studied at the Sorbonne. One evening, when they'd been comparing notes about university life, he had talked about his degree in terms of it being a personal goal. Didn't he understand that it was the same for her, too?

She didn't know whether it was because for once they'd failed to communicate, or because Jeb was seated across the dance-floor from her, but she found that she felt tense. Was it her imagination or was he watching her? She glanced up sharply, meaning to put him down with a cold stare. But, far from taking any notice of her, he was smiling at the woman seated opposite him, his mouth quirking attractively.

Gwenyth had formed only a brief impression of sophisticated glamour when his companion had entered the dining-room with him. Now, studying her in more detail, she saw that her sister hadn't exaggerated. His girlfriend was stunning.

In her late twenties or early thirties, she was supple

and poised, chic in the way that Wallis Simpson had been chic. Her strapless mulberry crêpe dress set off her perfect figure, and only a very beautiful woman could have worn her hair in such a short style. For some reason Gwenyth took an immediate dislike to her.

At that moment Jeb's gaze interrupted hers. His brows drew together, a quizzical light that was almost amusement coming into his eyes. A tinge of colour in her face that he had caught her staring, she meant to glance away. But somehow his intensely blue eyes seemed to hold hers like a spell, making tension vibrate the air dangerously between them.

Too late she realised that the defiant tilt of her chin was a dare to his virility. Murmuring something to his companion, he stood up, obviously intending to come over to the table where she sat with Marc. Possibly he would have done so anyway to make some sarcastic comment, but she wished furiously that she'd resisted the temptation to look in his direction.

Catching sight of him, Marc commented wryly, warning her unnecessarily, 'Jeb's heading this way. And I thought we'd picked the perfect place to enjoy the evening!'

As though greeting old friends, Jeb halted at their table. In a dark suit, he appeared urbane, but she was reminded uneasily of a pirate inspecting a prize he intended seizing as his own as he made a leisurely appraisal of her.

'We seem fated to meet,' he observed mockingly.

'I'd hardly call it fate,' Marc answered with sarcasm. 'It's more a one-off coincidence. The last time we met was at the quarry, and that was pre-arranged.'

A knowing smile touched the corners of Jeb's mouth for an instant. With a slight lift of one dark brow, he silently enquired why Gwenyth hadn't told her fiancé how they had met by accident on the beach.

She curled her fingers tightly into her palms. The reason why she hadn't mentioned it was because there hadn't been the opportunity. Or was it because briefly, when Jeb had kissed her, she had responded to him? The honesty that lay at the core of her nature forced her to admit that she hadn't told Marc because she felt guilty. And it was Jeb who had prompted that guilt.

'Well, it's nice to see you back, Marc,' he went on easily. 'A contest always goes a little flat when one of the participants quits the ring.'

Obviously nettled by the jibe, Marc said with cold anger, 'I did not quit.'

'That's right. You were summoned by your superiors.'

Since strolling over to their table, Jeb hadn't addressed a single comment to Gwenyth. The way he was talking, she might have been some captive slave-girl to be won, not a woman in charge of her own destiny who had already made her choice regarding the man she wished to marry.

Thinking it was high time she reminded him of that, she said, irritation in her voice, 'You seem to forget, Jeb, that I have a say in all this.'

'I don't forget for one minute,' he corrected her, his masculine gaze shifting to her lips.

She blushed as his insolent eyes made her recall

his plundering kiss. His mouth quirked at her inability to flash back with a reply. Inclining his head mockingly at the two of them, he strode away.

'He's as arrogant as ever!' Marc exclaimed under his breath. 'Who's the woman with him?'

'I don't know and I don't care.'

'Well, you're right about one thing,' Marc said grimly. 'He doesn't give up.'

'Why don't we go somewhere else?' she suggested.

More than anything else the complacent glitter in Jeb's blue eyes had unnerved her. He was like some poker player, a player who, far from bluffing, held all the aces in his hand.

'Why should we?' Marc frowned. He enclosed her fingers in his warm clasp. 'No, we're staying right here.'

Taking a deep breath, she gave Marc a little smile of agreement, resolving not to let Jeb's presence disturb her. Her fiancé was right. Why should they allow him to spoil their evening? Yet, despite her determination, she found it hard to relax.

She was glad that couples were now swaying to the slow, nostalgic music. They gave her the protection of being partly screened from Jeb. It was annoying, but even against her will she found that he drew her gaze. The magnetism of his personality was inordinately powerful. She disliked him, but she had to acknowledge the fact.

She watched as his companion shook a cigarette out of the packet, the light catching the gold bracelet which adorned her slim wrist. As she placed the filtered tip between her lips, Jeb picked up the folder of matches on the table. He struck one of them and the woman leaned forward gracefully towards the yellow flame. Their eyes locked for an instant before she moved back, blew smoke, and smiled at him through it.

She had merely lit a cigarette, yet as a piece of cool flirtatiousness it had been perfect. Gwenyth, while outwardly unruffled, felt a hot blaze of irritation at the display.

'What are you thinking?' Marc murmured, a smile in his voice.

'I. . . I was watching the dancing,' she said, quickly denying that her attention had been focused on Jeb.

'The band's very good,' Marc commented.

It was some time later that he suggested they should dance. The small floor was quite crowded. Marc was a good dancer, just as she was, but for once she found that she had to concentrate on following his steps. The unsettling touch of Jeb's gaze prevented her from floating naturally with the music.

Annoyed by it, when the tempo changed to a faster beat she swept her fiancé a dazzling smile. He caught hold of her hand, spinning her towards him. No one would have known, watching the easy gracefulness of her movements, that she was aware in every inch of her of the dark-haired man seated on the other side of the dining-room, whose enigmatic gaze was pinned on her.

It was during the next number that suddenly she seemed to find her natural sense of rhythm. When at last the dance ended she was laughing and slightly breathless. She joined in the appreciative clapping and, as she did so, she saw that Jeb's table was empty. Her sense of relief was swiftly followed by a little stab of triumph. If Jeb had hoped to unsettle her tonight, he must have left the hotel a disappointed man.

Her cheeks were flushed prettily and, putting a hand to her hair to smooth a wisp in place, she said, as they went back to their table, 'I need to make a few running repairs. I won't be long.'

'If you're planning to touch up your lipstick, I'm only going to kiss it off the moment we're alone,' Marc warned softly.

Returning his smile, she picked up her bag and then made her way between the tables towards the exit. As she crossed the elegant black and white tiled foyer with its bursts of greenery and club armchairs, she thought that the Plas yn Dre hotel would make a lovely venue for her wedding reception, if Marc agreed.

The ladies' room was up a flight of thickly carpeted stairs. She reached the wide landing, pushed open the door and slipped inside. Standing in front of the large mirror checking her make-up was Jeb's sophisticated dinner companion. She gave Gwenyth a long, hard look, her green eyes feline and cold.

Pretending to be unaware of it, Gwenyth began to neaten her hair. The woman opened a little compact of blusher. Deftly she flicked a sable brush over her cheekbones, the hint of beige-whisper colouring enhancing her striking looks.

In a voice that was languid and insolent, she asked, 'Isn't one man enough for you?'

Taken completely by surprise, Gwenyth faltered, 'I beg your pardon?'

The woman snapped the compact shut. Her gaze flicking arrogantly at Gwenyth, she repeated, 'I said, isn't one man enough for you? You've been eyeing

Jeb all evening, although I take it you're with your fiancé, since you're wearing an engagement ring.'

The unprovoked attack robbed Gwenyth of speech for an instant. Simmering with affront, she managed, 'Now listen, Miss. . .'

'Lisa Van Danzig,' the woman supplied arrogantly.

'I'm not trying to steal Jeb Hunter from you,' Gwenyth informed her icily. 'Far from it!'

Lisa smiled faintly, a false, sweet smile. 'That's just as well,' she replied, her voice lightly taunting, 'because you wouldn't succeed. Jeb needs a woman as a partner, not a little girl.'

Gwenyth's eyes sparked. Refusing to continue with the bitchy exchange, she pivoted sharply and left the room. There was anger in her step as she descended the stately staircase.

To heighten her temper, Jeb was lounging in one of the armchairs, his lean body as graceful as a panther's at rest. Rubbing a thoughtful finger against his chin, he studied her with piratical blue eyes as she crossed the foyer. The very complacency of the gesture maddened her. It was as if he was utterly certain that he would add her to his list of conquests in the end.

Before she had time to think of the wisdom of engaging in confrontation with him, she paused by his chair and began heatedly, 'You really have a knack of ruining everything I plan! On top of having to sit by while you jeer at my fiancé yet again, I now have to be insulted by your insufferable girlfriend.'

Jeb rose to his feet. His tone dry and faintly mocking, he answered, 'I'd be very surprised. What exactly has Lisa just said to you?'

Her lips parted and then closed again as she

realised that she couldn't repeat the accusation without pandering to his masculine ego. 'I suggest you ask her,' she retorted.

She went to sweep away from him, but he snatched hold of her by the wrist. Like a wild thing suddenly trapped, she insisted in a panic, 'Take your hands off me!'

'Strange, isn't it, the way your pulse leaps whenever I touch you?' he taunted.

'You're utterly despicable!' she flashed.

His grip on her tightened. Tension crackled between them like high-voltage electricity, dangerous, unseen and unpredictable. Jeb's attractive mouth thinned.

'If I were, I'd have told your fiancé how sweetly you make love on the beach when the mood takes you,' he said.

'You rat!' she breathed, crimsoning. 'I hate you!'

Sardonic amusement came into his eyes as he noted her angry blush. Releasing her, he said in a voice resonant with latent power, 'Hate me all you want, but you'll be mine in the end.'

'Never!'

Never, never, never, she repeated the words to herself as she spun away from him. And yet, for all her angry defiance, she was trembling as she went back into the dining-room.

CHAPTER SIX

RESTLESSLY, Gwenyth turned on her side and dragged her pillow further down under her cheek. A few minutes later she turned once again. With a short sigh she flickered her eyes open. It was small wonder she couldn't get to sleep, she thought, not with Jeb Hunter on her mind.

His implacable pronouncement at the hotel this evening had shaken her, the more so because fate seemed to be conspiring against her, forcing her path to cross with his. Yet for all his unrelenting determination, nothing he said would come true, she kept telling herself. She would never be his. She hated him more than any man on earth!

She lay staring wakefully up at the ceiling before finally throwing back the covers impatiently. Pulling on her blue silk wrap, she went over to the window and drew aside the curtain to look out.

Not a light twinkled across the valley. Against the night sky, the mountains rose up as towering shadows, brooding and remote. To gaze out into the velvety darkness at the austere ranges which seemed to be waiting, as they had waited for centuries, was quietening. Yet she was still unable to put Jeb out of her mind.

The love spoon he had given her lay in the middle drawer of her dressing-table. She took it out, anger welling up in her afresh as she noted the way his initials were entwined with hers. She would have stoked the Aga cooker in the kitchen with his love spoon had Marc not insisted that they keep it, saying that some day they'd recount the story behind it to their grandchildren.

She stared at the token of courtship and challenge a moment longer and then, almost as if she was afraid that it could somehow put a jinx on her feelings, she thrust it back into the drawer. Perhaps a cup of hot milk would help her to unwind. At this rate she was going to get no sleep at all.

The house was absolutely still as she silently went downstairs. She was surprised to notice that a light was burning in the drawing-room. Thinking it must have been left on accidentally, she crossed the hall and walked into the room. Her hand went automatically to the switch and then stopped as she saw her father sitting by the fireplace, staring into space.

Wearing a maroon dressing-gown over his pyjamas, he looked much older than fifty-five. It jolted her a little. There were furrows between his greying brows as he puffed pensively at his pipe. Ricky lay close by the wheel of his chair.

'Dad?' she began questioningly. 'What are you doing up at this hour?'

'Hmm? What?' Derec looked at her blankly. He'd been so deep in thought he obviously hadn't heard her come in. Rousing himself quickly, he said with a smile, 'So you couldn't sleep either?'

She nodded. Seeing the notepad on the coffee-table that was covered with his figuring, she said, 'It's a strange time to be doing calculations, isn't it?'

Derec reached out and picked up the notepad. He slipped it casually into the pocket of his dressing-gown. 'Some people count sheep,' he said, joking in his warm, Welsh voice. 'I add up figures.'

Gwenyth sat down on the sofa, concern in her amber eyes. 'Dad, don't fob me off,' she said quietly. 'You're worried about something. Mother knows you're not your usual self, and I've noticed it, too. There's nothing the matter with your health, is there?'

Her father patted her hand. 'I've got two women fussing over me now, have I?' he said.

'More than fussing,' she insisted. 'I love you, Dad, and I'm worried about you.'

'You've no need to be. I'm as fit as a fiddle.'

'But something's wrong,' she persisted. 'Dad, please tell me. What is it?'

Rubbing his fingers wearily across his forehead, he said, 'I've had a few difficulties to cope with recently.'

'What sort of difficulties?' she probed.

'It's something I hadn't reckoned on. I've some financial problems.'

'Not serious, surely.'

'I'm afraid so,' her father said. He drew a deep breath, before stating heavily, 'When I sold the quarry to Jeb three years ago, I invested most of the money in Smith-Courtland.'

'But. . .but that's the investment group that's been in the news recently, the one that's gone into liquidation through alleged fraud,' she said in a shaken voice.

Her father nodded, his face bleak. Steeling herself for still worse to come, she asked, 'How much have you lost?'

'I don't know exactly,' he said grimly. 'The first figures released by the liquidators suggested that the investors would get back seventy per cent of their money. Now that figure seems likely to be less than twenty per cent.'

'What are you going to do?' she asked in a hushed voice. 'I mean, you'll have some income, won't you?'

'It will be months before all the investigations are completed. The liquidators hope they may be able to pay a small sum back to investors some time next year, but in the meantime the house will have to be sold.' He sighed wearily. 'As for Sian going to university—well, that's a long way off. Perhaps I'll be able to manage it somehow.'

Gwenyth gazed at him in dismay. She felt almost dizzy with the shock of the financial catastrophe. Her parents had lived in the house for almost all of their married life. She thought of the love and care her mother had lavished on it, the garden she had tended over the years. And then there was her sister's education. Sian had set her heart on studying to be a vet—five years of training, she reminded herself.

'I've got a bit of money saved,' she said. 'Would it help?'

A sad smile flickered briefly in Derec's eyes. 'You're a good girl, Gwenyth,' he murmured.

'It's not enough to make any difference, is it?' she guessed miserably.

'Even if it were, I wouldn't take it.' His right hand balled into a fist on the arm of his wheelchair. 'A man should provide for his family, not the other way round. Failing you all is the hardest thing about all this.'

'Of course you haven't failed,' she protested.

'Haven't I?' he said, a wry twist to his mouth. 'The truth is, I'm half a man, a cripple in a wheelchair who can't even invest his money wisely.' Taking a deep breath, he went on, 'Don't say anything about this to your mother. I'm still hoping my accountant will come back with better news. The lowest ebb's the turn of the tide.'

Gwenyth nodded, summoning up a frayed smile as she kissed him goodnight. She wanted to believe what he said, that the situation wasn't as desperate as it seemed. But the newspaper she fetched from the study and took upstairs so that she could read the detailed financial section told her that, if anything, her father had underplayed things.

Sitting on her bed, she hugged her knees with her arms. There had to be some solution, she thought, as she chewed her lip. Hope momentarily kindled in her eyes. Marc was a financial expert. Surely he'd know what to do.

Needing to confide in him, she slid off the bed, meaning to talk to him at once even though it meant waking him. And then she hesitated. What could he suggest that she hadn't already thought of?

She remembered how scathing he had been about investors who had lost badly in the stock-market crash. Would he view her father in the same unsympathetic light, as a speculator with more money than sense? He would be tactful enough not to say it, but she would know from the quirk of his eyebrows that it was what he thought.

Besides, even if Marc were to offer her father a loan, how could he possibly ever pay it back? Her heart contracted painfully as she remembered her father's harsh words of self-condemnation. He was a proud and sensitive man who had always provided well for his family. To have to accept charity from his son-in-law would break him.

Her eyes began to burn and then, suddenly, she lifted her head. The answer was so wonderfully simple that she could have laughed shakily with relief. Jeb had told her that he was looking for someone to supervise the tourism project at the quarry. With his knowledge of the industry, her father was the perfect man for the job.

For the first time she wished she was on a friendlier footing with Jeb. Then she could have made the suggestion quite casually. As it was, she didn't know exactly how she was going to go about it. But one thing was for sure. She wasn't going to confess to him that her father had invested in Smith-Courtland. No appeal, however emotional, would sway a man as ruthless as Jeb.

Butterflies fluttered in her stomach as, after breakfast the next morning, she slipped into the study to phone him. She'd spent a sleepless night debating the best method of approach. She wasn't going to find it easy to be civil to him after their exchange last night, but it was vital that she arrange to see him.

She walked round behind the mahogany desk and sat down. She found Jeb's number and then, taking a deep breath, she picked up the receiver. Nibbling at her fingernail, she waited for him to answer. A faint frown appeared between her eyes as the ringing tone continued. Surely on a Sunday morning she would catch him at home. Unless. . .

Her lips tightened as angrily she wondered if the reason she was getting no reply was because Jeb had spent the night with Lisa at Blaen Wern. And then she started as at that moment the study door opened unexpectedly.

'I didn't realise you were making a phone call,' her mother apologised for interrupting.

'I'm not!' She replaced the receiver with guilty haste. 'I mean, there's no answer. I'll. . . I'll have to try again later.' Quickly she attempted to conceal her confusion. 'Are you looking for your glasses?' she asked as she searched the top of the desk, knowing that she was blushing and hoping that her mother wouldn't notice.

'How did you guess?' Catrin laughed. 'I always seem to be mislaying them.'

'They're here on the bookcase.'

'So that's where I left them,' Catrin said, before asking, 'Are you and Marc coming with us to church this morning?'

'I'll ask him,' Gwenyth answered.

St Teilo's was a pretty church. It was built in the twelfth century, but the original structure dated back five centuries earlier. Wooden pillars carved from native oak lined the nave and transept, while light filtered through the stained-glass windows, making coloured patterns on the stone floor.

Gwenyth took her place between Marc and her mother in the family pew. The previous day had seen the start of a flower festival in the church and, as well as the carnations and sweet-peas on the altar and round the pulpit and lectern, flowers were massed at the sides of the nave. Cleverly arranged, they illustrated the Biblical themes depicted in the stained-glass windows.

Marc commented on them. As, quietly, she turned to hear his whispered remark, she glimpsed Jeb's tall figure three pews ahead of her on the other side of the aisle.

Her surprise at seeing him in church meant that
she failed to catch what Marc was saying. Luckily,
since the organ began to play at that moment, a nod
made an adequate answer. She opened her hymn
book, finding that as she sang she was staring at the
back of Jeb's dark head and the strong line of his
shoulders. He needs to be in church, she thought,
remembering his total lack of ethics!

Marc observed the direction of her gaze. The last
reverberating chord of the final verse of the hymn
died away and, as the congregation sat down again,
he whispered wryly to her, 'There seems to be no
getting away from Jeb Hunter.'

'No, there doesn't,' she agreed in a murmur, her
voice too low for him to hear the troubled note in it.

When the service came to an end the church slowly
emptied. Gwenyth knew practically all the congregation. She'd been home just over a week, ample
time for the news of her engagement to have spread,
and everyone wanted to offer her their good wishes
and to meet her fiancé.

Standing outside the church chatting with the
various groups of people, at some point she and
Marc became separated. Jeb was standing talking
nearby. Catching sight of her, he strolled over to join
her. It was an ideal opportunity for her to arrange to
meet him later, but the antagonism that stirred in her
as she looked up into his arrestingly masculine face
made her momentarily forget how important it was
that she be polite to him.

'What are you doing here?' she began accusingly.
'I've never seen you attend a service before.'

'I've been coming to church for some time now on

a Sunday,' he said. 'I told you, I mean to be accepted
here.'

'I might have guessed. . .' she started, and then
swallowed the rest of her words. To state scathingly
that it was typical of him to have some ulterior motive
was hardly going to help her cause.

'You might have guessed what?' Jeb enquired with
a mocking lift of a dark brow.

'That you'd go about any aim determinedly,' she
amended, her tone less hostile, even if there was
defiance in the tilt of her chin. 'When I phoned you
this morning and got no reply, I'd no idea it was
because you were on your way here.'

Quizzical blue eyes narrowed on her face. 'Why
did you want to phone me, Gwenyth?'

The way he spoke her name made it sound like a
caress. It sent a strange little shiver tracing over her
skin. Bristling with him a little in spite of herself, she
answered crisply, 'It wasn't about anything personal,
if that's what you're thinking. There's something I'd
like to discuss with you. I was wondering if I could
call in at the quarry some time tomorrow.'

'I'll be in Manchester all morning, and in the
afternoon I've got a series of meetings,' he told her.
'But you're welcome to call round at my house in the
evening.'

Out of the corner of her eye she noticed her fiancé.
A grim look on his face, he was heading towards
them. With no time to state that she'd prefer to meet
him at the mine offices another day, she agreed
quickly. 'Yes, all right. At your house.'

'Here comes lover boy,' Jeb commented mockingly,
a glimmer of contempt in his blue eyes. 'Would you
like me to include him in the invite?'

'No!'

The masculine line of his mouth twitched with amusement at her panic-stricken answer, and she coloured hotly. Damn him, she thought, realising too late that somehow he had anticipated her reaction.

'Then I'll see you tomorrow,' he said, touching her lightly on the shoulder as if they were friends parting.

Together with the taunting inflexion in his voice, it made anger spark dangerously in her eyes. She was staring after him as he strode away when Marc said at her elbow, arrogance in his tone, 'Jeb soon cleared off when he saw me coming.'

Irritable, she swung towards him, and the defeat flickered in her eyes. How could she possibly explain to Marc how threatened Jeb made her feel when she couldn't explain it to herself?

The problem of working out how she was going to call round at his house without telling Marc where she was going ensured that she remained on edge for the rest of the day. When Monday came she still hadn't found a solution. If only she could be open with him, she thought despairingly. But it simply wasn't possible.

If she said she was calling on Jeb, he would demand to know why. Her first impulse had been to confide in him about Smith-Courtland. But on reflection she was glad she hadn't. After the promise she had given her father, it would have been a breach of trust. Not only that, but her hope was that her father would be offered the job without ever knowing that her intervention had anything to do with it.

She bent to fasten Ricky's lead. 'If only everything wasn't so complicated,' she murmured feelingly.

The dog gazed up at her with sympathetic brown eyes, understanding her mood if not her words.

'Are you taking Ricky for a walk?' her mother asked as she bustled into the kitchen.

'I thought I would,' she said with a sigh.

Catrin gave her a look that was tinged with concern. 'If you've something on your mind, talking often helps,' she suggested kindly.

'I'm fine,' Gwenyth protested, forcing a smile. 'What makes you think I'm not?'

'Well, a walk's a good way of mulling over a problem.' Catrin didn't press the matter. 'Is Marc going with you?'

'He's engrossed in a Maigret thriller. I don't want to disturb him.'

Few cars passed her to disturb the sunny quietness as she walked. Crickets chirped in the long grass by the roadside. In the distance the angular summits were tinted with a bluish hue that blended softly with the pristine summer sky. Like an amphitheatre, they enclosed the lower hill slopes that were trimmed with gorse and bramble.

She walked some way before branching off down a farm track through a field to the river. The stepping-stones which spanned it gleamed white and dry in the warm midday sunshine. She jumped nimbly from one to the next while Ricky splashed across further upstream, shaking himself vigorously as he reached the other side.

Picking up a stick, she threw it for him, continuing with the game as they crossed the wide meadow. It wasn't until they came to the car park on the edge of town that she put him back on the lead. If it hadn't

been for the problem that was worrying her, she
would have enjoyed the walk as much as Ricky.

She was passing the newsagent's when Lisa came
out of the shop, her huge Rottweiler at her side. The
big dog growled alarmingly the moment it saw Ricky,
who barked back, the hair on his neck bristling.

'Detmar, heel!' Lisa shouted as the dog bounded
down the steps on to the pavement.

Ignoring the shrill command, the Rottweiler sprang
upon Ricky with a terrifying snarl, sinking its teeth
deep into Ricky's neck. Ricky yelped with pain.
Afraid of the savage Rottweiler, but even more afraid
for Ricky, Gwenyth grabbed hold of it by its collar,
pulling at it with all her strength.

'For goodness' sake!' she cried out to Lisa. 'Call
him off, can't you?'

'Detmar, come *here*!' Lisa ordered, the firmness in
her voice marred by a slight edge of timidity.

It might have made a difference if, instead of
keeping a cautious distance from the two dogs, she'd
caught hold of Detmar by the scruff of the neck. But,
as it was, her dog paid no heed to her. Snarling, he
continued to shake Ricky, who let out a high-pitched
howl which changed into a piteous panting sound
deep in his throat as he struggled to free himself.

Gwenyth's arms were aching from wrestling with
Detmar and, terrified that the Rottweiler was going
to kill her dog, she shouted in angry despair, 'Get
help if you can't do something!'

At the same moment, hearing the commotion, the
portly owner of the newsagent's came out, broom in
hand. 'Let go, you brute,' he thundered, threatening
Detmar with the broom before pushing it into the
dog's chest.

Tugging desperately at the Rottweiler's collar, Gwenyth was scarcely aware of the red Range Rover that drew to an abrupt halt by the kerb alongside her. Jeb swung out of the driving seat, rounding the bonnet with long, purposeful strides.

Gwenyth glanced up. Thankful that he had stopped his car to help, she called out in a choked voice, 'Please, Jeb! Quick!'

'Lisa, get the back door of my car open,' he instructed.

She moved quickly to do as he had said, while the red-faced and out-of-breath shopkeeper stepped back, only too glad to let someone else try to separate the dogs. Jeb's mouth thinned into a determined line as he grabbed hold of the huge Rottweiler. Slowly he prized the brute's jaws open with his strong man's hands.

Ricky immediately pulled free, trembling in every leg as he cowered away from his attacker. Feeling equally shaken, Gwenyth knelt down beside him.

'It's all right, Ricky. It's all right,' she murmured.

She patted him gently, watching while Jeb dragged the Rottweiler towards his car and ordered him inside.

Lisa ran a hand through her short, carefully styled hair. 'My!' she exclaimed with an airy little laugh. 'That was quite a drama!'

'Quite a drama?' Gwenyth repeated incredulously as she stood up, her eyes sparking. 'It was terrifying!'

'You ought to keep that dog of yours on a lead, Miss Van Danzig,' the shopkeeper put in sternly. 'He's a menace.' Turning to Gwenyth, he asked kindly, 'Would you like to come inside the shop and sit down for a while? You look very pale.'

'I'm OK,' Gwenyth insisted. 'Thanks, Mr Jones. You were wonderful.'

'It's Mr Hunter you should thank.' He shook his head. 'Without him, heaven knows how we'd have got the dogs apart.'

Taking the broom, he went back into the shop. As he disappeared inside, Lisa asked spitefully, 'Are you going to make a play for Jeb's sympathy, too?'

Gwenyth still felt tremulous with reaction. As she was shaken, and upset because Ricky was hurt, Lisa's bitchiness lit the fuse to her temper. 'You really are something else!' she exclaimed angrily. 'You're not fit to have charge of an animal. That dog of yours is completely out of control!'

'That's not——' Lisa snapped back and then, seeing Jeb approach, she broke off, her lashes fluttering as she burst into injured tears.

Jeb put a protective arm around her shoulders. 'Hey, what's this?' he said gently, brushing her temple with his lips. 'You mustn't cry.'

Lisa mastered her tears enough to accept his handkerchief and to look up at him with shimmering green eyes. 'I'm sorry. It's just that Gwenyth. . .' Her voice caught in a sob.

Jeb kissed her again. 'Sit in the car and I'll be with you in a minute.'

She nodded, giving him a brave little smile while, simmering, Gwenyth watched the display.

'There was no need to reduce Lisa to tears,' Jeb stated when they were alone on the pavement.

Stung by the injustice of the remark, she flashed

with angry sarcasm, 'Your protectiveness is most touching.'

Blue eyes narrowed on her face. 'Do I detect a slight note of jealousy?' he drawled mockingly.

The taunt was too much for her. Forgetting that she was in his debt for coming to her help so effectively, she erupted, 'What a typically conceited remark! It's not surprising I hate you!'

'Do you?' he asked softly, a wealth of meaning in his charismatic voice.

She blushed at his deft reminder of the passion with which she had kissed him. Jeb's mouth quirked. Bending down, he gave Ricky a friendly pat before parting the hair on his neck. The dog whimpered, but stood still obediently while he inspected the savage bite.

'If I were you, I'd take him along to the vet this evening,' he advised.

'I don't need you to tell me how to take care of my dog,' she retorted stormily. 'In any case, I'm calling round to see you this evening, or had you forgotten?'

'No, I hadn't forgotten,' he said, straightening so that once again he towered above her.

Their eyes locked, tension quivering along her nerves. His reply seemed almost portentous and, hating the electricity that vibrated between them constantly, she dragged her gaze away from his.

Once her engagement ring had seemed an adequate protection from Jeb. Now suddenly she felt vulnerable. She only hoped, as she walked off with her slim shoulders squared, that he didn't guess it.

CHAPTER SEVEN

WITH a glance in her rear-view mirror, Gwenyth signalled that she was about to make a left turn. Ahead of her was the long rhododendron-lined drive which led to Jeb's house. Apprehension made her mouth feel dry. So much rested on the outcome of her meeting with him.

She was glad that the stretch of main road was empty as she turned off it. In view of the fact that she was engaged to Marc, anyone who knew her could be forgiven for thinking it a little strange that she should choose to go calling on Jeb alone on a summer evening.

Immediately she chided herself. It was silly to be feeling so miserably guilty. She didn't like keeping a secret from Marc, but it wasn't as if this was some kind of illicit assignation. She was merely doing what she had to in the best interests of her family.

She parked her car, picked up her shoulder-bag from the passenger seat, and then hesitated as she looked at the white Regency-style house that rose up, shaded by the graceful larch and pine trees in its grounds. Like everything else Jeb owned, it was impressive.

Four wrought-iron columns formed a veranda along the front of the house and supported an elegant balcony. The upstairs sash windows were flanked by blue shutters, as were the french windows which gave on to the veranda. Beautifully kept lawns sloped down to meet the curving drive, and the flower borders were a mass of colour.

A low wall separated the drive from the salt marshes beyond, which with their water channels and tall, tassled reeds were a paradise for wildlife. In the gentle evening sunshine the river gleamed like a sheet of polished pewter, the blue-tinged mountains which rose up on either side of it reflected darkly in its smooth surface.

Taking a deep breath in an attempt to steady her nerves, Gwenyth got out of the car. She opened the rear door for Ricky, who climbed out stiffly, wagging his tail a little.

'I suppose we may as well get it over with,' she murmured to him as though he were an ally.

With the dog at her heels, she made an attractive picture as she walked towards the house. Her boldly patterned skirt was long and full, drawing attention to slim ankles and pretty sling-back sandals. The shade of turquoise in it was matched perfectly by her short-sleeved silk blouse. The rather severe cut flattered the youthful line of her breasts, while her long, burnished hair was kept in place by a chic twist that suited her features.

It was because she was so dreading this meeting that she had taken pains to look her best. But now she wished she hadn't. She didn't want to look attractive for Jeb. She decided that she would have felt safer wearing sackcloth.

Reluctantly, she went up the steps on to the veranda, paused a second to gather her courage, and then rang the bell. Jeb didn't answer immediately and, impatient because she was tense and on edge, she was about to press the bell again when the door opened.

Her pulse fluttered in response to the tall, virile figure who stood in front of her. A slight tinge of colour came into her face as Jeb's blue eyes narrowed hawkishly on her for an instant.

'Hello, Gwenyth. Come in,' he began lazily, standing back for her to enter.

'Thank you.' The terse note in her voice was the result of nerves. Determined to appear poised and at ease, she went on, 'It's a beautiful evening, isn't it?'

'Lovely.' It was obvious from his tone that he found her trite observation amusing.

Her amber eyes sparked, but just as quickly she brought her temper under control. There was nothing to be gained by flaring up with Jeb. It was crucial that, whatever her feelings, she keep the tenor of this meeting polite and formal.

The shrewdness in Jeb's gaze told her that her restraint hadn't gone unnoticed. Obviously interested by it, he motioned her towards the open door to the lounge. 'Make yourself at home.'

She acknowledged his invitation with a small, cool smile, and walked ahead of him into the spacious room. Apart from the view over the river, it looked completely different from when she had been in it last, over three years ago.

Jeb had had it decorated in complementing tones of beige and moss-green. Large, comfortable, modern armchairs were placed facing the windows. They blended in surprisingly well with the antique items of furniture in the room.

She noted the collection of Davenport china displayed in the Edwardian corner-cupboard. A fine

bowl, also Davenport, stood on an unusual art nou-
veau table, while the painting on the chimney breast
was by the Victorian artist MacWhirter.

The previous owner of the house, whose wife had
been an interior designer, had gone to great trouble
to furnish the lounge in Regency style with nothing
out of period. It irked Gwenyth a little to have to
admit it, but she found that she preferred the room
now that Jeb had put his masculine and characterful
stamp on it.

She sat down in one of the armchairs. The palms
of her hands felt clammy, and she used the pretence
of smoothing her skirt to wipe them. The atmosphere
in the room seemed charged and incalculable with
the knowledge that she and Jeb were completely
alone.

Ricky had wandered into the middle of the room
and would have settled down on the Chinese rug
had she not clicked her fingers gently and pointed
beside her chair. As the dog came to her obediently,
Jeb mocked, 'Did you bring Ricky with you for
protection?'

Her action had been prompted by defensiveness,
and it was with difficulty that she ignored the jibe.
Keeping her voice cool, and giving Ricky a pat, she
said, 'I've just taken him to see the vet.' Which was
where Marc, who luckily hadn't offered to come with
her, thought she was now.

'He seems very subdued,' Jeb observed, as Ricky
dropped to his haunches alongside her chair.

'What do you expect after the way that brute of a
dog attacked him this afternoon?' she asked.

'Are you blaming me?' Jeb enquired with an edge
of irony, amused by her flash of antagonism.

Annoyed with herself for flaring slightly, she answered, 'Of course not. I was only too thankful that you happened to be driving through the town.' Uncertain how to broach the topic of the tourism project, she went on, 'The vet's given him an injection of antibiotic together with something to take the swelling down. He says Ricky should be a lot better in the morning.'

'Good,' Jeb commented. He indicated his whisky glass, which stood beside a collection of papers on the coffee-table. 'I'm having a drink. Will you join me?'

She sensed that she was going to need all her wits about her to secure the job for her father, and she didn't particularly want any alcohol to cloud her thinking. Yet to refuse Jeb's hospitality would look pointed and unfriendly. 'I'll have a Tia Maria,' she said.

She watched him as he walked over to the drinks cabinet. He was as relaxed as she was tense. Everything about him, she realised, from his pantherish tread to his forceful personality, contrived to make her feel vulnerable.

'I expected you to ask for a Benedictine,' he remarked.

'Am I that predictable?' There was a faint shading of hostility in her tone.

'On the contrary, but I think I know a little about your tastes.'

There was an intimate note to his voice. It disturbed her. She glanced up into his eyes as she took the glass he handed her, meaning to dispute his statement. Instead, as their gazes locked, electricity seemed to flicker along her nerves, chasing the words from her mind. Afraid of the powerful awareness between them that she couldn't analyse, she lowered her eyes quickly, conscious that her heart was beating erratically.

'You're very pretty when you blush,' Jeb observed.

'I'm not blushing,' she denied coldly.

'What's the matter?' he asked, his voice softly taunting. 'Don't you like compliments?'

'Not from. . .Not especially.'

Jeb smiled faintly. The conversation wasn't going at all the way she wanted it to. Since it never did when she was with him, she might have guessed that it wouldn't.

He sat down in the armchair opposite her, his long legs staking out a claim on the carpet. Incapable of attempting to make small talk any longer, she decided to be direct.

'The reason why I've come here——' she began and then broke off, interrupted by the ringing of the telephone.

'Excuse me while I answer that,' Jeb said, getting to his feet.

She gave a slight nod of assent, outwardly all poise, while inwardly she sighed with frustration. Why did the phone have to ring now, just when she had steeled herself to begin?

From the tone of Jeb's voice it was obviously a business call. His manner was that of a man used to being in command. He was good, she thought ruefully, resenting him for it.

Leaning back in her chair, she tapped her fingers silently on the arm, watching him covertly as he stood with the window behind him. The evening sunlight that shafted into the room gleamed on his black hair. Virility seemed to be stamped into every line and plane of him. It was there in the proud set of his dark head, his broad, muscular shoulders, his stance which bordered on the arrogant.

His white shirt and impeccably cut navy suit made him seem more than ever to belong to the hard, swift-moving business world of power and profit. For an instant the sun went in. Then it appeared again, brightening the colours in his Paisley silk tie which showed conservative good taste.

Her gaze drifted upwards to study his masculine features. Modelled in light and shadow, the rugged angles of his swarthy face looked harsh and uncompromising. She noted the strong line of his jaw and the astute grooves etched between his dark brows.

As if sensing her covert study Jeb glanced at her, his blue eyes alert and speculative as he brought the phone call to a conclusion. Hurriedly she looked away, but not before she had seen his mouth curve briefly with faint, cynical amusement.

She reached for her liqueur glass and took a sip of its contents, wishing furiously that, instead of having to feign cool composure, she could march out of his house. His subtle mockery invariably nettled her, but this evening, with her nerves stretched taut, it riled her more than usual.

Jeb replaced the receiver. 'I'm sorry about that,' he stated. 'What were you saying?'

He sat down again in the armchair opposite her, loosening the knot of his tie as he did so before unfastening the top button of his shirt. An instant ago his appearance had been faultlessly urbane. Now, with his tie loosened, she was somehow acutely aware of the primitive pull of his raw, masculine charisma.

She moistened her lips and began, 'I wanted to talk to you about the tourism project. Have you appointed anyone to take charge of it?'

Jeb raised his glass to his lips, giving her a considering look. 'No, not yet,' he told her before swallowing a mouthful of whisky.

She clasped her hands together tightly in her lap. Keeping her voice deliberately casual, she said, 'I was wondering if you'd thought about Dad for the job. He knows the business inside out, and he's had plenty of experience with public relations.'

'Your father's been semi-retired for the last three years.'

'Yes, I know,' she answered. 'But he would never have retired in his fifties if it hadn't been for the accident. He's far too young and active in mind. I'm sure if you asked him you could persuade him to take the position.'

She scarcely seemed to breathe as she waited for Jeb to answer. She knew that she had put her suggestion to him well, but would he consider it?

'I probably could persuade him,' he agreed, rubbing a thoughtful finger along his chin.

Her heart leapt with hope. Failing to note the tigerish glint in his alert blue eyes, she continued, strenghtening her case, 'I'm sure it would be good for the company, and the appointment would be popular with the work-force.'

Jeb set his whisky glass aside. Almost certain that he was going to agree, she clenched her fingers in suspense. But, instead of answering her immediately, he studied her for a moment before asking, his tone almost conversational, 'How much has your father lost in Smith-Courtland?'

For a moment she stared at him. She'd been so sure of success that for an instant her mind refused to adjust to the fact that he knew of her father's financial predicament. Dismay echoing through her, she faltered, 'What?'

'I said, how much has your father lost in Smith-Courtland?' he repeated evenly. 'I take it that's why you're here.'

Her eyes darkened. Success had seemed within her grasp. Now it had been snatched away from her. 'How do you know?' she breathed accusingly. 'Who told you?'

'Your father mentioned some while ago he'd invested with them. Presumably, for you to be here this evening, he's lost heavily.'

'He. . .he's lost some money.' The reluctant admission was forced out of her.

'Which is why you've come to me,' Jeb summarised.

Resentment sparkled in her amber eyes as she looked at his strong, masculine face. The very relaxation of his body as he lounged in the chair antagonised her. Instinct told her that Jeb would never find himself in the same position financially as her father. With a gift for making money, he was always two moves ahead on the checker-board of business.

She knew that both his parents had died when he was young. His success had been achieved completely on his own. She grudgingly admired him for that, while hating his streak of hardness. But, desperate though the situation was, she refused to plead with him. With a defiant lift of her chin she said,

'Yes, that's why I've come. You need someone to take charge of the tourism project, so why shouldn't that person be Dad? But if you have someone else in mind, it won't be the end of the world. It's true my father needs money, but, if the job goes to someone else, there are other solutions.'

'Such as?'

'Dad can sell the house.'

'It's a possibility.' Jeb shrugged. 'But you've got to live somewhere and you won't save a lot on running costs. That aside, have you thought about how your mother will feel about moving? It won't be easy for her to see strangers living in her home.'

Gwenyth bit her lip. 'Mother would do anything to help Dad. In any case, they could move right away from Bron-y-Foel.'

'It would be very lonely. All their friends are here,' Jeb reminded her. 'And then there's inflation to consider. Selling the house may generate income in the short term, but, taking a longer view, your father could find himself even more hard-pressed in a few years' time than he is now.'

To her concern she realised that he was right. Standing up, she paced restlessly towards the fireplace. 'Moving's only one option,' she countered. 'I can get a job to help.'

'I thought you were getting married and going to live in France with Marc.'

There was an edge of sarcasm to his voice and she retaliated in kind. 'It is possible to find work in France.'

'Yes, if Marc allows it,' Jeb mocked. 'Though, from what I gather, he believes that a woman's place is in the home.'

'Marc may be a little old-fashioned, but he'll let me work if I want to.'

Jeb quirked a sceptical dark brow at her. Annoyed, she looked away. She might have guessed he wouldn't miss the slight note of uncertainty in her tone.

'You mean you're prepared to support your parents for the rest of your life?' he said. 'It's certainly very noble.'

'All right,' she flashed angrily. 'It's an impractical idea. But I could contribute for a time.'

Jeb rested a casual elbow on the arm of his chair. 'You seem very alone in all this,' he observed. 'I find that puzzling. Your fiancé's rich. Why haven't you asked him for help?'

'You know damn well why I haven't!' There was a catch of emotion in her voice.

'Yes,' he confirmed as he stood up and came towards her. 'Because your father's too proud to accept charity.'

Her throat tight, she looked up at him. She hated having to appeal to Jeb, but she had no choice. 'I've racked my brains trying to think of an answer,' she said huskily, 'and you're my last hope. This job would be a lifeline for Dad. But that doesn't alter what I've said about his being ideally suited to it. You know that as well as I do.'

Jeb's gaze, level and direct, held her pinned, his blue eyes unfathomable. 'I *could* offer him the job,' he agreed.

'Please, Jeb. I'd be so grateful.'

'*How* grateful?' he asked, a suave brutality in his voice.

For an instant her ears seemed to ring, everything

in the room, except the tall, arrogant figure who stood in front of her, spinning out of focus. Colour flamed in her face. His meaning was as clear to her as if he had said the insulting words out loud. In a voice that trembled with cold rage she said, 'Are you suggesting——?'

'Not suggesting,' he cut in. 'I'm stating my terms.'

Anger was so fierce in her she was almost trembling with its force. 'You unspeakable cad!' she spluttered. 'Do you really think I'd sleep with you when I'm engaged to Marc?'

Jeb's mouth twitched, as though he found her white-hot fury amusing. Totally master of the situation, he said calmly, 'You have two alternatives: to throw yourself on Marc's charity, or to share my bed.'

Her palm itched to connect with his swarthy cheek in a resounding crack. But, angry as she was, she somehow didn't dare strike him. Clenching her hand at her side, she snapped, her eyes molten-hot, 'Never!' A force-field alive with sexual tension seemed to vibrate the atmosphere. Needing to escape from it, she whirled away from him, swinging back to confront him as she exploded. 'Good grief! When I tell Marc about this. . .how you've had the nerve to proposition me, he'll——'

'I'm not propositioning you,' Jeb cut in sardonically, his face set in uncompromising lines. 'I'm asking you to marry me.'

She stared at him incredulously. Her mouth was dry as she tried to assimilate what he had said. 'You. . .you can't be serious!' she breathed.

'I'm perfectly serious,' he stated. He stood, tall and arrogantly male, making no move to cross the space that separated them. Yet there was a menacing sense of purpose in him. It showed in his craggy jawline and the narrowness of his unwavering gaze. 'Marry me, and I'll see that your father gets the job.'

'You must be out of your mind,' she declared. Vehemently, she reminded him, 'I'm engaged to Marc.'

Jeb strolled towards the coffee-table. Picking up his whisky glass, he finished his drink, strong throat muscles flexing as he swallowed. 'Break it off,' he said negligently. 'It's easily done.'

'I won't break it off,' she flashed in defiance. 'I love Marc.'

'Then your father doesn't get the job. It's as simple as that.'

A cold shiver seemed to trace down her spine as she realised the untenable position she was in. Her voice slightly unsteady, she accused, 'This is blackmail! You're blackmailing me!'

'Call it what you will——' he shrugged. '—but I intend having you as my wife.'

For a numbed instant she stared into his face. Drive and determination were etched into every masculine feature. She paled a little, shaken by the discovery that when she had judged him to be ruthless she hadn't known the half of it. The very thought of being his wife filled her with fear, agitation and confusion. She spun away, needing to clear her mind of the disturbing picture of what it would be like to share her most intimate moments with him.

With her back to him, she said in a husky voice, 'I'll never marry you! Never, do you understand?'

In her state of turmoil she didn't hear his predatory tread as he approached her. When his hand traced her neck lightly she started, shying away like a highly strung filly.

A glitter of masculine satisfaction in his eyes at her reaction to his caress, he reminded her, 'You have very little option. Not if you're as concerned about your family as you claim to be.'

He was hemming her in. Snatching at any argument that might save her, she snapped, 'Why do you want to marry me when you know I hate you?'

'If you remember,' he drawled, 'you suggested that, to be accepted in the community, I marry someone local. Having thought it over, I came to the conclusion that your advice was very sound.' That her own words should be responsible for the trap she was in was the ultimate irony. He continued sardonically, 'Your family is Welsh and has lived here going back generation upon generation. When our son is born, even if I'm still called the foreigner, he certainly won't be.'

'You think I'm going to give you a son!' she breathed in angry disbelief.

'Not immediately. I'm prepared to let you finish your degree, if that's what you want, before we start a family.'

'How magnanimous of you!' she flashed sarcastically.

Jeb studied her with speculative detachment. 'I'm waiting for your answer,' he said calmly.

She dug her nails into her palms, refusing to let him see that her hands were trembling. There was no point in making an appeal to him. She saw that now. Her eyes burning with resentment, she said in a shaken voice, 'You planned this all along, didn't you, right from the moment you gave me the love spoon? You knew Dad had invested in Smith-Courtland. Not only that, but you made sure I knew about the tourism project. You must have guessed I'd come to you for help.'

'You could have tried Marc instead,' he jibed. 'Or is Marc a dead loss in that field too?'

'What do you mean, "in that field too"?' she demanded angrily.

'I mean,' he taunted with quiet ferocity, 'that if Marc satisfied you sexually, you wouldn't be trembling to be seduced by me.'

A blaze of fury engulfed her. Swinging up her hand, she slapped him with all the force she could muster. There was the sharp crack of the blow and then an ominous, pulsating silence.

His eyes glittering, Jeb snatched hold of her wrist. Across one lean cheek the marks of her fingers showed dull red. Afraid of what she had done and of the dangerous force she had unleashed in both of them, she snapped in panic, 'Let go of me!'

'When I'm ready,' he muttered harshly, pulling her hand against him.

The contact with his lean body seemed momentarily to knock the breath out of her. In desperation she tried to hit out at him again and, as she did so, Ricky rose from his haunches, a warning growl coming from his throat.

'Quiet!' Jeb ordered. The single word was enough to check her dog.

Unable to twist her hand free, Gwenyth turned her head aside frantically as Jeb's mouth moved closer. 'No——!' she gasped as he caught hold of her chin with determined fingers.

Her angry protest was lost as his lips found hers.

The hands that had snatched her captive were brutal, and she expected Jeb's kiss to be equally savage to punish her for having slapped him. Instead, it was both passionate and plundering.

A tremor shook her, a hot, nameless hunger stirring inside her. She could feel the size and strength of his powerful man's body against every inch of hers and, terrified of the feelings he was kindling in her, she thudded her fist against his shoulder. But there was no escaping the arms that arched her against him.

Her heart was shaking her with its poundings, a frightening dizziness making her mind reel. No one, not even Marc, had ever kissed her like this, making her feel ravaged and invaded. A soft sound murmured in her throat as his palm caressed her back, pressing her breasts to the hard plane of his chest. An agonising surge of pleasure went through her and, in desperation, she twisted free.

She didn't know how long the kiss had lasted, but even now that it was over her spinning world refused to right itself. Her legs felt so weak that, had Jeb allowed her to break away from him completely, she would probably have staggered.

His blue gaze searching hers with glittering intensity, he asked, his voice ragged with desire, 'Are you still going to deny what's between us? You want me as much as I want you. Admit it.'

She stared back at him, her eyes huge in her flushed face. She was breathing as hard as he was, shattered by the discovery that, encouraged by the sensual persuasion of his mouth, her hatred could ignite into passion.

Huskily she denied it, fear of her treacherous

senses fuelling her anger, 'There's nothing between us!'

'Isn't there?' he said gratingly.

She caught a glimpse of his face as he bent his head again, the saturnine lines of it intensified with passion. She pushed against his chest, but resistance was useless. Jeb kissed her long and intimately, the passionate demand of his mouth sending wild tremors of fire dancing along her nerves. Her hands, that had gone to repulse him, crept towards his neck, her fingers tangling in his dark hair.

A maelstrom of desire had her spinning. Scarcely realising what she was doing, she began to kiss him back. Always his blatant, indomitable maleness had antagonised her, causing sparks to fly between them of late. But now, suddenly, even the memory of the way they had fought was a powerful aphrodisiac, bringing her slim body alive with a feverish madness.

Jeb's mouth that plundered hers evoked from her a response so acute, she thought she was falling. It was only when she felt the softness of the cushions at her back that she realised he had swept her off her feet and lowered her on to the sofa. His weight pressed her down, his hands touching her throat, her breasts and hips as he caressed her.

A blaze of erotic sensations made her tremble even as, at the back of her mind, the confused knowledge stirred that this was wrong. 'No,' she moaned pleadingly.

She started to struggle, but he caught hold of her hands, placing them flat against the warmth of his chest.

'Touch me,' he commanded raggedly.

'No. . .Please. . .' she whispered, tears starting to her eyes as she fought to clear her feverish senses.

He silenced her protest, his mouth claiming hers in a deep, hungry kiss. Involuntarily her fingers tightened on his shoulders. Jeb's hand, which had slid beneath her blouse, cupped her breast before gently stroking her, making hot shivers of pleasure trace over her skin. Shocked by her feverish response to him, she broke the kiss, and then gasped, her fingers digging into his back as his thumb brushed her taut nipple.

Jeb raised his head and, in horrified realisation of what she was allowing, she pushed him away, almost sobbing with shame as she stumbled to her feet. The pins had come loose from her chignon, and the weight of it brought her long, glossy hair cascading around her shoulders as she fumbled in distress with the buttons of her blouse.

Jeb stood up too, breathing harshly as he caught hold of her by the shoulders. 'Marry me,' he said huskily.

She shook her head. In a tormented whisper she breathed, 'I can't!'

'I think you've just proved very conclusively that you can,' he said, taking hold of her left hand.

Realising that he intended removing her engagement ring, she protested in alarm. 'No! Jeb, don't! I. . . I haven't agreed to anything yet.' She whirled away from him, her face flushed as she pleaded agitatedly. 'Please, you must give me time to think.'

'The offer isn't a standing one,' Jeb said harshly. 'If you want me to help your father, you'll say yes now.'

She pivoted back to face him. Devastated by the response she had given to him, she was in no state to marshal her defences. Angry tears in her eyes, she capitulated, 'All right. Since I've no choice, I'll marry you.'

A glitter she assumed was triumph flickered in Jeb's eyes. Taking her in his arms, he bent his head, his mouth teasing hers in a light kiss.

'I don't think you'll find it such a sacrifice,' he mocked softly.

She blushed hotly at his reminder of how willingly she had kissed him. Looking up at him, she said in a voice that shook with hatred, 'Am I free to go home now?'

Jeb's mouth tightened a little. But there was no evidence of anger in his tone, only a shading of sarcasm as he said, 'You're in no fit state to drive home. If you were to have an accident, I'd never forgive myself. I'll drive you and we can tell Marc the good news at the same time.'

'You bastard,' she hissed. 'If I can face the prospect of a lifetime as your wife, I can certainly face telling Marc that I can't marry him. And I don't need you to drive me home!'

Calling to Ricky, she swept towards the door.

CHAPTER EIGHT

SIAN ran up as Gwenyth drove slowly along the gravelled drive and drew to a halt in front of the house.

'How's Ricky?' she asked anxiously as she opened the back door to let the dog out. Patting him, she went on, 'You've been gone much longer than I expected.'

'I. . . I had a long wait at the vet's, but Ricky's fine.'

'Does the vet want to see him again?'

'Yes, in two or three days' time, just to make sure he's OK.'

'That's not so bad then, is it, Ricky?' Sian fondled one of the dog's silky ears as she spoke to him. Straightening up, she announced, 'Oh, by the way, Dad and Marc have gone up to the golf house. You've only just missed them. I told Marc you'd join them when you got back.'

Gwenyth swallowed against the tightness in her throat. She didn't feel she could face Marc, not right now. But sooner or later she was going to have to tell him their engagement was off. She flinched at the prospect. Yet what right did she have to wear his ring after the way she had acted with Jeb?

Marvelling that she could sound so normal when she was so shaken and ashamed, she said, 'I'll have to neaten up a bit first. I feel rather untidy.' The result of Jeb's devastating lovemaking, she thought, stung with remorse.

She went inside the house and up the stairs. Her hand shook slightly as, sitting on her bed, she brushed her hair. She went on brushing it even when it streamed smooth as a cascade of silk over her shoulders. It was as if, dreading all action and wanting to avoid thought, she was afraid to stop. Glancing up, she saw her reflection in her dressing-table mirror. Her eyes were darker than usual, revealing her distress. But, much as she wanted to, she couldn't hide in her room forever.

Agitatedly, she paced over to the window. The last of the evening sun was catching the upper slopes of the mountains, creating patches of brilliant green among the brooding summits. Sheep grazed placidly on the lower pastures. The very tranquillity of it all mocked her inner turmoil.

'Damn you, Jeb Hunter,' she breathed in anger.

She might have agreed to be his wife, but she would hate him forever for forcing her to choose between her father and Marc.

The clubhouse was crowded when she arrived, and it took her a moment to locate her fiancé. He was standing at the bar, chatting to Huw Davis, the transport manager at the quarry and a keen golfer.

'Hello, darling,' he began. 'You've been a long time.'

'It's a woman's privilege to be late. Isn't that right, Gwenyth?' Huw joked. 'Anyway, now that you're here, what will you have to drink?'

'I'll have a mineral water,' she said mechanically.

'You devil,' Huw teased, commenting as the

barman poured it for her. 'Your fiancé plays a very good game of snooker. He's just beaten me hollow.'

'But I doubt if I'd beat you at golf,' Marc said affably. 'Derec tells me you have a handicap of one.'

'I've been playing a long time,' Huw said.

Handing her mineral water to her, he guided Gwenyth across the room to where his wife sat talking to Derec, together with another couple who were also members of the golf club.

Wishing desperately that she hadn't come, she sat down and, with a forced smile, said hello to everyone. Stupidly it hadn't occurred to her that the atmosphere of conviviality at the clubhouse would make it impossible for her to say to Marc that she wanted to go somewhere quiet so that they could talk.

She twisted her engagement ring wretchedly on her finger, periodically adding a token comment to the conversation at their table. More people had come in, having finished their round of golf now that the light had failed, and the clubhouse was full of talk, laughter and smoke. The painful throbbing in her temples wasn't helped by either the chatter or by having to keep up the façade that nothing was wrong.

It was some while later that Marc leaned closer to her to suggest, 'Shall we make a move?'

She had spent the last half-hour longing to leave. But, now that the moment had come when she was going to have to tell Marc that she couldn't marry him, she clutched at the first excuse she could think of to delay the inevitable. 'I think Dad's still enjoying himself.'

'I was planning on walking back,' Marc murmured meaningfully, giving her hand a squeeze. 'It's such a lovely night. It seems a pity to waste it by waiting for a lift.'

She bit her lip. 'All right,' she said huskily. Standing up, she put a slim hand on her father's shoulder, interrupting him to say, 'We're leaving now, Dad. We'll see you back at the house.'

After the babel of talk and laughter in the clubhouse, the night seemed wrapped in quietness as they walked down the sloping road. Stars shone in the dark, lofty sky, and the mountain air was laced with the faint, elusive fragrance of spruce and pine.

'You've been very quiet all evening,' Marc commented.

'I. . . I have a headache,' she faltered.

'Why didn't you say?' he demanded. 'We could have left earlier.'

Because I'm a coward, she thought, hating herself. Anger stirred anew inside her. It was because of Jeb she was going to have to hurt Marc, whom she loved.

'It's nothing,' she insisted, her voice tense. She gathered her courage. 'Marc——'

'It's quite chilly,' he observed, cutting across her as he so often did. 'Would you like my jacket, or is an arm round you enough to keep you warm?'

'No!' She side-stepped away from him to avoid his caress. Despairingly she said, 'I. . . I mean I'm all right.'

'You don't sound it.' There was an edge of irritation in his voice.

She stopped. Looking up at him, she said huskily, 'Marc, there's something. . .there's something I've got to tell you. . .'

'*Alors!*' he exclaimed impatiently. 'Why so serious?

You're not still fretting about that damned dog of yours, are you?'

'He's not a damned dog,' she corrected him sharply, her nerves stretched to breaking-point.

'Temper!' Marc said with a frown. 'I know you're fond of the animal, but keep it in perspective. In my opinion, you needn't have bothered to take him to the vet.'

'Which shows how much you know about animals——!' she retorted and then broke off, a wave of hopelessness washing over her. The last thing she meant to do was to get into an argument with Marc. 'I. . . I'm sorry.'

He didn't comment on her apology and, after a moment's strained silence during which they walked on, Gwenyth said, in a voice that tremored slightly, 'Marc, I've been thinking.'

'About your course, I suppose?' he said drily. 'You don't want to give it up.'

She clenched her nails into her palms, forcing herself to say the words. 'It's more than that. Marc, I'm sorry, I'm terribly sorry, but I can't——'

Sternly he interrupted, 'Listen, *chérie*, if we're going to have a happy married life together, you're going to have to learn a bit of give and take.'

As he was speaking, a car drew up beside them. Lowering the window, Howell Evans, one of the members of the golf club, called out, 'Would you like a lift to save you walking?'

'We may as well for all the use we're making of a moonlit evening,' Marc muttered for her hearing only. Raising his voice, he said, accepting the offer, 'Thanks, it's kind of you.'

They were home in under five minutes. Mr Evans

insisted that it was no trouble to turn the car, and swung into the drive to drop them right outside the house.

'That's good timing,' her mother said, smiling as they entered the drawing-room together. 'I've just made a pot of coffee.'

'I could do with a cup,' Marc said, sitting down, the faint lines etched between his brows the only sign of his displeasure with Gwenyth.

'How about you, dear?' Catrin asked her.

'No, not for me, thanks,' she said. Summoning up a smile, she hid her misery and frustration. 'I'm tired. I think I'll go to bed.'

Worn out with emotional tension, despite the regrets and self-recriminations that nagged at her, she finally drifted off to sleep. For an instant, waking late the next morning, she couldn't locate the cause of what was bothering her. And then it all came back. To save her father from financial ruin she had agreed to marry Jeb.

But it wasn't a decision she had wanted to make. Colour came into her face as she remembered the tactics he had used to persuade her. She had never believed in sexual chemistry, yet how else could she account for the power Jeb had over her senses?

Even to think of the way he had caressed her last night was to feel a quiver go through her. In an agitated whirlwind, she discovered that she'd committed herself to something she couldn't possibly go ahead with. She loved Marc. He made her feel safe and protected, not threatened by emotions she could neither control nor analyse. She wanted to help her father, but she wanted to be Marc's bride as well.

At that moment it didn't matter that it was an

impossible combination to achieve. She'd think of
some way out of this nightmare. She had to. But first
she desperately wanted to make up with Marc. Till
Jeb had appeared on the scene, they'd never had a
wrong word. She was torn in two between concern
for her parents and her sense of loyalty to her fiancé.
But love was supposed to conquer all. If that was
true, surely everything would work out in the end.

In a more optimistic frame of mind she went
downstairs. Sian was in the kitchen, fetching the
copy of *Macbeth* she'd left on the work-top. As
Gwenyth walked in she joked, 'Lazy-bones. What
time do you call this?'

'It's only ten to nine,' Gwenyth protested with a
laugh, before teasing her back. 'Besides, look who's
talking. You're going to be late for school.'

'I can walk to school in ten minutes.'

'Are you sure? I'll run you along if you want.'

'No, it's OK.' Sian thanked her with a smile as she
shrugged on her blazer.

The percolator was still hot and Gwenyth poured
herself a cup of coffee. She was surprised that Marc
wasn't in the kitchen. He was an early riser, but he
liked to linger over breakfast, reading the newspaper.
Wanting to talk to him, she asked Sian, 'Where's
Marc?'

'He's gone to the quarry.'

Gwenyth gave her sister a swift, alarmed glance.
'What?' she faltered.

'Jeb phoned this morning to say he had something
to discuss with him,' Sian explained. 'I don't know
what it's about.'

Gwenyth's heart jolted with dismay. She had only
agreed to marry Jeb under duress. But how would

Marc know that, when Jeb told him—or the fact that she'd since changed her mind?

'Whose car did he take?' she demanded urgently.

'Mother's. Why? What's the panic?'

'I'll tell you later,' she promised recklessly as she dashed out of the kitchen.

She snatched up her car keys from the hall table and ran outside, ducking into her Metro before pulling away with a roar of acceleration. Desperate to catch Marc and explain things before Jeb spoke to him, she drove fast. But even as she turned in through the quarry gates she guessed she was going to be too late.

By a stroke of luck there was a free parking bay close to the main entrance of the mine offices. She swung into it and screeched to a halt. Hurrying into the building, she whipped along the thickly carpeted corridor to the outer office which connected with Jeb's inner sanctum.

His secretary was at the filing cabinet, fetching a file, as she burst in. Delyth glanced round, moving to intercept Gwenyth as she headed for the door opposite.

'Mr Hunter's in a meeting. You can't——' she began in protest.

'Can't I?' Gwenyth muttered mutinously.

She flung open the door, pausing just inside, her dramatic entrance severing the conversation. Jeb was perched on his desk, arrogance and power in every line of his body. A dark brow quirked in her direction.

Ignoring him, she glanced swiftly at Marc, the burning contempt she saw in her fiancé's eyes as he

met her gaze momentarily robbing her of the power
of speech.

'I'm terribly sorry, Mr Hunter,' his secretary apologised. 'I simply couldn't stop her.'

'That's all right, Delyth.' Addressing Gwenyth, he
said pleasantly as his secretary went out, closing the
door behind her, 'In fact, it's probably just as well
you've come.'

Marc's gaze raked her chillingly. '*Mon dieu*!' he
exclaimed in a voice that bit with condemnation.
'You've played me for a right fool! It was Jeb all
along, wasn't it?'

'No!' she protested. 'That's not true! I don't know
what Jeb's said, but I can ex——'

'Can you?' Marc broke in savagely. 'Then why
don't you start by explaining what you were doing at
his house last night?'

'I. . . I went there because——' she began before
breaking off. Her eyes smarting, she swung accusingly to Jeb. 'Just what have you told him?' she
demanded.

'The truth,' he answered, coming towards her.
'That you've agreed to marry me.' His blue gaze
mocked her as he slid his arm around her waist so
that they faced Marc as a couple. 'I guessed you
might not know how to break it to him. That's why I
decided to do it for you.'

Furious with him, she began tempestuously, 'You
had no——'

Marc's voice, filled with bitter scorn, overrode her
own before she could finish. 'And I thought last
night you were trying to tell me you didn't want to
give up your course! You've played this very cleverly,
haven't you? All the time pretending you had no

interest in Jeb, saying how much you disliked him, and I believed you! Lord, it's rich.'

Fighting the strangling tightness in her throat, she pleaded, 'Marc, listen——'

'So you can tell me some more lies?' he snapped, slashing her with his contempt, as he reminded her, 'You were taking Ricky to the vet, you said. You wanted to burn Jeb's love spoon. You were going to give him short shrift if he dared call round to see you. Instead, what happens? You go sneaking off to keep a lovers' tryst with him.'

'No,' she insisted. 'It wasn't like that!' She brushed a distraught hand across her forehead. Her meeting with Jeb hadn't been an assignation. But she couldn't protest her innocence when she only had to remember the passion that had flared between them to go hot with shame. A tremor in her voice, she went on, 'You don't understand.'

'I understand only too well, but it's a wonderful act you put on,' Marc sneered, 'the modest girl from the very proper Welsh background, the girl who couldn't kiss her fiancé in case her parents came into the room. Well, it didn't stop you cheating on me with your lover behind my back, did it, you little——'

'That's enough!' Jeb cut in with quiet ferocity, the chiselled lines of his face as hard as a fist.

Marc's mouth tightened, but the ring of steel in Jeb's voice wasn't something to be ignored. Biting back the insult, he stated sarcastically, 'Then there's nothing left to be said.'

'Marc, wait!' she implored as he strode to the door. Jeb's hand was against her back. Without realising it, she had been grateful for its support. But now she moved forward. 'I know how it looks, but——'

'But what?' Marc demanded coldly, the icy scorn in his eyes freezing her. 'Why not admit it? You're in love with Jeb. Well, I wish you joy of each other.'

He walked out of the office, slamming the door behind him. Feeling numbed, for an instant she was incapable of any action. She knew he wouldn't listen to her, yet even so she took an uncertain step towards the door.

The quiet authority in Jeb's voice stopped her. 'Let him go.'

She pivoted to face him, her flaming hair whirling about her shoulders. Tears glistened in her amber eyes. She struggled to master them, far too proud to break down and cry in front of him.

He was standing by his desk, tall and ruggedly male, his gaze scalpel-sharp as he studied her. There was not one flicker of regret in his chiselled features for the way he had broken her and Marc up. A riot of emotions, all of them violent, rose up inside her at his utter ruthlessness.

'I hope you're satisfied with what you've done this morning,' she said in a choked voice.

Jeb folded his arms across his chest with arrogant detachment. 'We made a deal,' he reminded her. 'It's fortunate that I'm a little more scrupulous about keeping my word than you are about keeping yours, or I could well turn round now and tell you that your father can whistle for the job.'

'I didn't want to hurt Marc,' she defended herself.

'I'm sure he'll survive,' Jeb said drily.

'That's exactly the sort of callous remark I'd expect from you!'

Her flash of temper appeared to amuse him. 'You ought to be grateful to me,' he mocked.

'Grateful!' she spluttered.

'If it hadn't been for me you'd have gone ahead and married that dogmatic egotist. Instead of appreciating you, he'd have forced you to conform to his notions of a meek little wife. In time he'd have turned you into as big a bore as he is.'

'And what are *you* going to turn me into?' she demanded sarcastically.

His masculine mouth quirked attractively. 'I wouldn't dream of changing you. You suit me the way you are, temper and all.'

'I didn't know I possessed a temper till I ran foul of you!' she retorted, sweeping on. 'You've made a prediction of what my life would have been like married to Marc. Well, now I'll make one of what yours will be like married to me. You're going to regret giving me that love spoon, because I plan to be the shrew of all time!'

'Then I'll just have to teach you to mend your ways.' Coming towards her, he tilted her chin up. His gaze shifted lazily to her lips, making her heart seem to skip a beat. 'Won't I?' he said, his mouth coming down on hers.

His kiss was a harsh, male caress. Her chance to try to escape had been before he had bent his head. The moment his lips were on hers it was too late. A shock of feeling went through her, rendering her helpless.

Quick to sense it, Jeb put his arms round her, bringing her body into a more intimate fit with his. The evidence of his arousal made her give a panicky moan deep in her throat. In response to it, Jeb's arms tightened. At the same time he deepened the kiss. Demanding, intimate and insatiable, it seemed to go on forever. When at last he raised his head, her lashes fluttered up and she stared at him with dark, bewildered eyes.

No matter how hard she tried to resist, Jeb only had to snatch her into his arms for her to respond as tremulously as some musical instrument in the hands of a master. How could she hate him, and yet be overwhelmed by sensations so hot and feverish when he kissed her that even now her pulse refused to steady?

Completely unnerved by the chemistry of attraction between them, she spun away. Struggling with her emotions, she stood by the window, keeping her back to him, her head slightly bowed.

'Take off the engagement ring you're wearing,' Jeb said on a husky note.

Her nerves tensed as in every inch of her she sensed him coming towards her. 'I've. . . I've nowhere to put it,' she said in a muffled voice as she did as he ordered. 'I rushed out of the house without my bag.'

Jeb swept her long hair aside. 'You can wear it on your right hand until you see Marc and give it back to him,' he murmured, his lips brushing her neck sensuously.

Suddenly his assault on her fragile emotions was too much. Her breath caught in a sob. Immediately, Jeb turned her to face him.

'Are you crying?' he demanded.

'No,' she said defiantly.

Her eyes were misted. Had they not been, she might have seen and been puzzled by the look of half-angry tenderness in his face. He caressed her cheek with his thumb, wiping away the dampness.

'They look like tears to me.'

The pain around her heart tightened unbearably. Right now, kindness from him was the last thing she could handle. Jerking away from him she snapped, 'Don't touch me!'

The hard line of his jaw clenched imperceptibly. A sardonic note to his voice, he said, 'I'll take you home and we can make it official.' Resentfully she didn't answer, and he observed, 'Your mascara's smudged.'

'What of it?' she flashed mutinously.

'If your father's not going to guess the noble sacrifice you're making on his behalf, you'd better fix it.' He nodded towards an unobtrusive door. 'There's a cloakroom through there.'

She was glad to be sparring with him again. Anger was strengthening. With a sarcastic, 'You're all heart, aren't you?' she headed in the direction he'd suggested.

In the privacy of the small, neat cloakroom she caught her trembling lower lip between her teeth. She mustn't think of the earth-shattering passion with which Jeb had kissed her, just as she mustn't think of Marc. There was no point trying to make sense of her feelings now.

She splashed cold water on her eyes and straightened her blouse. Her hand trembled slightly as she smoothed her hair. She was only surprised to see in the mirror that she looked as presentable as she did.

When she came out of the cloakroom, Jeb was standing looking out of the window, hands in the pockets of his trousers. Hearing her step, he turned, hawkish blue eyes narrowing in inspection. As ever, his gaze had only to linger on her to remind her that she was a woman.

Lifting her chin defiantly, she asked, 'Do I pass muster?'

'Very much so,' he drawled. 'Are you ready?'

'As ready as I'll ever be,' she conceded resentfully.

'Then let's go.'

His hand at her elbow, he escorted her from his office. She was conscious of his advantage over her in height and of the breadth of his shoulders. The awareness was disturbing, bringing a smouldering light into her eyes. She would not permit herself to be sexually attracted to a man she felt such enmity for.

As they passed Delyth's desk, Jeb paused to say, 'I'll be out of the office for an hour or so. Tell anyone who calls I'll get back to them this afternoon.'

'Yes, Mr Hunter.'

As his secretary finished speaking she flicked a curious look at Gwenyth, obviously trying to work out what had taken place behind the closed door of Jeb's office this morning. Not that she would have long to wait to find out, Gwenyth thought wryly, wondering what people would make of it when it became known that she had broken off her engagement to Marc in order to marry Jeb.

They would doubtless conclude that Jeb had swept her off her feet. And, to add injustice to the monstrous irony, she would probably be deemed a minx while Jeb was admired for his bravado.

In hostile silence she proceeded along the corridor with him. As they crossed the wide foyer, he said with dry mockery. 'Try not to look as if you're about to be sold into the white-slave trade.'

'It's a fate one worse,' she retorted, stabbing him an inimical glance. 'I'm being forced to marry you!'

A cynical smile touched the corners of Jeb's mouth. 'Was it university or charm school you went to while you were in France?' he enquired.

With an effort she stopped herself from rising to the taunt. Since in every fencing match with him she invariably came out the loser, there was no point in flashing back with an answer. Amusement in his eyes at her restraint, he swung open the door for her.

As he guided her towards where his Range Rover was parked, she said in a childish attempt to assert her independence, 'I don't want to leave my car here. You drive and I'll follow you in my Metro.'

'Are you thinking of making some wild dash for freedom?' he mocked.

'It would be pretty pointless, wouldn't it?' she snapped. 'Since you hold all the winning cards, I've no option but to go ahead and marry you.'

'Gracious even in defeat,' he jibed. Opening the passenger door of his Range Rover for her, he stated, 'I'll get one of my men to drive your car round for you later.'

Defeated on all fronts, she got in. Jeb made no attempt to communicate with her as he drove out of the quarry. She flicked a glance at him. The strong lines of his profile were impassive. They gave her no clue as to what he was thinking.

Her gaze travelled from his swarthy features to his strong hands, which rested capably on the steering-wheel. She knew what it was to be caressed by those hands. With the thought, the full impact of the fact that she was going to be his wife seemed suddenly to hit her. She glanced away hurriedly, staring out of the window as she tried to bring her agitated emotions back in check.

'Since this is supposed to be a love-match,' Jeb mocked with deft irony as they drew to a halt outside her house, 'may I suggest you stop sulking?'

'I'm not,' she denied icily, adding sarcastically, 'I'm saving the sweet loving act for when my parents are present.'

Intensely aggravated by his arrogant smile, she got out of his car. He strolled leisurely round the bonnet to join her, his black hair gleaming in the sunlight. She was determined that she wouldn't show any sign of weakness in front of him. Yet inwardly she shrank from the further bitter words she knew she must expect when she handed back her engagement ring to Marc.

'Shall we go in?' Jeb said.

'No. . .' Suddenly unable to sustain her spirited pretence, she confessed, 'I. . . I don't think I can face this.'

'You can with me beside you,' Jeb returned. 'That's what love's all about.'

His jibe was too much for her. Her eyes flashing and her colour heightened, she exploded, 'Lord, you make me angry!'

The masculine line of his mouth quirked with amusement. Grazing her cheek lightly with his finger so that her eyes sparked more furiously still, he said, 'Temper becomes you, my sweet. While you're still blushing like the bride-to-be, let's tell your parents the good news.'

CHAPTER NINE

GWENYTH shied away from Jeb's insolent caress. To have to feign that she was in love with him was the last straw. Yet, as he had pointed out, she had no choice. Simmering, she swept ahead of him into the house.

Her mother glanced up and, pausing in what she was saying to her husband, rose to meet them as they entered the drawing-room. 'Hello, Jeb,' she said with her customary friendliness, before asking in puzzled concern, 'Gwenyth, maybe you can tell us what's going on? Marc's packed and left without a word of explanation.'

Derec pivoted his wheelchair around as he took up the story. 'He stormed into the house about half an hour ago. The next thing we knew there was a taxi pulling up outside and he was bundling his things into it. What's made him leave so suddenly?'

Twisting her fingers together, she began, 'Well, you see. . . I. . .'

'Gwenyth's changed her mind about marrying him,' Jeb interposed to convey what she was having difficulty in expressing. As he spoke he put a hand against her back, making her start slightly. Her gaze flew to his face. She might be forced to tolerate his proprietorial touch in front of her parents, but she meant him to understand that it would be a different matter when they were alone together. Paying no heed to her silent message, Jeb went on calmly,

'Obviously, Marc felt there was no point in staying on.'

'I never dreamed he'd just pack his things and go,' Gwenyth said huskily.

Catrin patted her daughter's arm. 'Darling, I'm sorry,' she said kindly. 'I know how you hate to hurt anyone, and it must have been very difficult for you to tell Marc. But it's better a broken engagement than an unhappy marriage.'

'Your mother's right,' Derec agreed. 'It will be hard on Marc for a while, but he'll get over it in time. Try not to feel too bad about it.'

'I do feel bad about it,' she admitted. She looked up at Jeb, a flash of rebellion in her eyes, which a moment before had been dark and earnest. 'But I had to break off our engagement because. . .'

Jeb took over from her. 'Because your daughter's done me the very great honour of falling in love with me.'

His gaze met and held hers. Used to veiled mockery from him, she was taken completely by surprise by the quiet, firm note of sincerity in his charismatic voice. Coupled with the powerful eye contact between them, it made her heart lurch alarmingly.

Did Jeb mean what he was saying? she wondered in bewilderment. Was it possible that he actually loved her? Immediately she was furious with herself for even entertaining the idea. She knew full well what Jeb's motives were in marrying her. He'd spelled them out very clearly. Damn him and his powerful, masculine charm, she thought stormily. It was small wonder he could fool her parents, when he could take her in as well.

Yet such was the chemistry between them that she

had to make an effort to free her gaze from his. With an attractive, reprobate smile, Jeb concluded, 'I have to admit I did everything in my power to win her.'

Catrin was the first to react to the news. Breaking the instant's stunned silence, she said, admonishing herself with a laugh, 'I don't know why I'm acting so surprised. I guessed Gwenyth was in love with you some time ago.'

'You guessed?' Jeb smiled. His dark brows lifted quizzically, but his blue eyes were sharp.

'When sparks fly between two young people the way they've been flying between you two of late, there's only one explanation for it,' Catrin answered.

'Well, you kept that dark, *cariad*!' Derec laughed.

'I thought you'd accuse me of wishful thinking,' Catrin said, smiling.

'I knew you weren't too happy about Gwenyth going off to live in France,' he agreed.

'That was selfish of me. Of course it's nice when your children marry locally, but what's important is their happiness.' Catrin's affectionate glance rested on her daughter. 'And that's what worried me. I only had to see the way you flared up just at the mention of Jeb's name to wonder if you weren't engaged to the wrong man.'

'Did she now?' Jeb said.

The note of humour in his voice roused hot anger in her heart, but she couldn't rise to the jibe because of her parents. Seething with her inability to flash back at him, she said with a forced laugh, 'Jeb, don't tease!'

'How can I help it? You're so teasable,' he answered, giving her a squeeze.

She felt that she would choke on his mockery. He

was not only enjoying her helplessness—he was exploiting it to the full. Observing the vibrancy between them, Catrin smiled and exchanged a fond glance with her husband, who quipped, 'Let me guess. The reason you recognised the signs of true love so quickly was because you were always so ready to spar with me when we were courting.'

'Now, Derec, we don't want to go down memory lane,' Catrin chided, actually blushing slightly. 'But my goodness, you had a cheek asking me to marry you the very first time we went out together!'

'A man ought to know his own mind,' her father stated. 'I think we share that in common, Jeb. Congratulations. I don't have my wife's intuition, and this has taken me completely by surprise, but I'm very pleased.'

'I'm so happy for you both,' Catrin put in warmly. She embraced Gwenyth and then kissed Jeb. 'In one way or another, it's been quite a whirlwind of a morning.'

'I suppose it has,' Jeb smiled, giving Gwenyth a tender look that was laced with mockery.

She glared back at him before hurriedly recollecting herself. There was a curious angry ache beneath her ribs. Sharp words would have eased it, but remembering that she was supposed to be in love she looked back at him mistily and vowed vengeance later.

'How about a glass of sherry?' Derec suggested. 'My mind immediately jumped to business when I saw you, Jeb. I'd no idea this was in the air.'

'As it happens, I do have a business matter to talk over with you.'

'Whatever it is, it can wait,' Catrin insisted. 'Now,

Jeb, what would you like? A Montillado or a cream sherry?'

'It's a bit early for me,' he answered as he sat down on the sofa.

'We'll have coffee then,' Catrin said.

'I'll give you a hand,' Gwenyth offered quickly, feeling that she needed a respite if the flawless act she was putting on was to hold up.

'There's no need, dear. I can manage.'

'It will give the men a chance to talk business.' As Gwenyth spoke she gave Jeb a sweet smile.

Her casual remark was full of hidden meaning. Understanding it, Jeb lifted his dark brows with faint mocking derision. For some reason, by reminding him of the terms under which she had agreed to be his wife she had succeeded in annoying him; in scoring a point in revenge.

They were all set now for confrontation the moment they were alone together, and the knowledge gave her an odd sense of satisfaction. Jeb was hard, ruthless and implacable. But for once she had needled him. It was a skill she intended fostering.

In the kitchen her mother gave her another quick hug. 'I was so afraid you wouldn't wake up to your feelings till it was too late,' she said. 'Marc was a fine young man, and very steady, but if you'd married him I think you'd have found him much too heavy-handed for you.'

Honesty forced Gwenyth to concede. 'He probably would have laid down the law a little.' But that was nothing compared to the way Jeb was curbing her freedom, she thought resentfully. Since she could hardly find fault with the man she was supposed to be head over heels in love with, she restricted her criticism to a mild, 'Though Jeb can be pretty firm as well.'

'Yes, but in a different way,' Catrin said as she filled the percolator. 'He has a very forceful personality, yet he's easygoing with it.' A twinkle of amusement came into her eyes as she confessed, 'I don't believe in matchmaking, but I have to admit I'd often thought what an excellent husband and father he'd make.'

Gwenyth didn't answer. It was infuriating to hear his praises being sung so lavishly. Head bowed, she began to butter some scones. Puzzled by her silence, Catrin gave her a speculative glance.

'You are planning on having children, aren't you?' she asked.

'Yes, of course,' Gwenyth said, colour coming into her cheeks at the thought of consummating the bargain she had struck with Jeb. Quickly she went on, 'But not immediately. Jeb says he understands I want to finish my degree first.'

'I think that's sensible,' her mother commented. 'It's nice to be a couple for a while before you have your family.'

She carried the tray into the drawing-room, and Gwenyth lifted the bowl of roses off the coffee-table so that her mother could set it down. Her father had lit his pipe. Slipping the box of matches back in his pocket, he asked, 'How do you feel about having me out from under your feet again, *cariad*?'

Catrin paused in pouring out. 'What plot have you two been hatching?' she queried playfully.

'I've asked Derec if he'd be interested in taking charge of the tourism project at the quarry,' Jeb explained.

'What project's this?' Catrin asked with interest. 'I didn't know you had any plans for developing tourist facilities at the quarry, Jeb.'

'Few people did,' he answered. His eyes met Gwenyth's as she handed him his cup. The glint of mockery in them made her long to tip the entire contents over him. 'It's a new development, but one which should pay off. The aim is to open some of the old workings to the public so that visitors can get some idea of what the quarries were like in the last century. It will be like a living museum, with a craft centre and miners' tramway, together with the usual tourist facilities of car park and restaurant.'

'It sounds most exciting,' Catrin said. Glancing at her husband, she went on, 'I can see why you'd like to be involved with it, but are you sure it won't be too much for you?'

'It's just what I need,' Derec stated. 'As a matter of fact, I was looking around for some type of consultancy work. I've had too much time on my hands of late.'

Gwenyth could almost hear the relief in his voice. It told her how heavy the burden of the collapse of Smith-Courtland had been for her father. Yet his reaction went even deeper than that. It was as if the prospect of working on a challenging and demanding project again had given him back his stature as a man.

'Well, this should certainly stop you staring into space the way you have been recently.' Catrin laughed.

Gwenyth, who had joined Jeb on the sofa for the look of things, felt him put his arm around her. He had exacted a high price from her in payment for his help, but he had honoured his word.

Turning the conversation back to their wedding plans, her mother asked them, 'When are you thinking of getting married? Have you set the date yet?'

Before she could answer Jeb said, 'Yes, we have.' His hand caressed her shoulder. 'Gwenyth wants a summer wedding, so we've decided on July.'

She wanted no wedding at all, and certainly not as soon as he was proposing. Feeling all the more rebellious because of the havoc his touch was playing with her senses, she glared at him. Immediately his fingers tightened on her shoulder, making her think better of protesting.

'As soon as that!' her mother exclaimed. 'But we're already in the second week of June.'

'We're not planning on a big wedding,' Gwenyth told her, deciding that if Jeb could fabricate what they'd discussed, so could she. There was no point in turning their wedding into even more of a sham than it was already. 'We want a simple ceremony with a very small reception afterwards, perhaps at the house.'

'That's something we can talk about later,' Derec put in. 'There's heaps of time.'

'Now, isn't that just like a man?' Catrin exclaimed. 'Here we are with six weeks at most to get everything planned, the invites printed and sent out, the church booked and Gwenyth's dress bought, apart from all the other arrangements that have to be made, and you insist that there's plenty of time!'

Her exasperated comment drew laughter from the others, albeit feigned from Gwenyth. The topic of the wedding dominated the conversation until Jeb stood up to leave.

Knowing it was expected of her, Gwenyth saw him out. As they crossed the hall, Jeb drawled, 'You put up a most convincing performance. It was a real joy to watch.'

'Oh, I'll play the loving wife in public,' she said, her amber eyes rebellious.

'And in private?' he mocked.

It was clearly nothing to him that she had no wish whatsoever to be his wife. She was merely the means to an end. Anger in her voice, she said, 'I mean to give you hell!'

'Where's your sense of gratitude?' he jibed.

'I shouldn't need to be grateful to you,' she flashed as they halted at the front door. 'My father was the man for the job all along.'

Jeb tilted her chin up. 'To think you were going to waste all that fire and spirit on Marc,' he taunted softly.

Knowing he intended kissing her, she breathed furiously, 'Don't you dare!'

Unable to fight him with her parents in the next room, she adopted a different line of resistance, willing herself to stay cold and passive as his mouth claimed hers. He might have outmanoeuvred her at every turn, but she was determined not to give in to the magnetism of sexual attraction between them. She had kissed him with passion for the last time.

When he raised his head, her eyes sparkled defiantly. She felt a little dizzy and off balance, but she had won.

'It's better when you kiss me back,' Jeb said lazily, brushing his thumb over her lower lip.

His caress sent a feverish shiver down her spine. Adamant that she would never give herself to him willingly, she answered with frosty insolence, 'Is it?'

'We'll have to try it again when we're alone.'

There was a sensual note to his voice. Coupled with the resolution in it and the dangerous electricity that crackled between them, it threw her into a panic.

'You really expect your pound of flesh, don't you?' she snapped.

His masculine gaze roved over her deliberately, lingering on the agitated rise and fall of her breasts before returning to her face. 'Down to the last ounce,' he answered.

She drew breath to flash back with a stormy answer and then checked her flow of words as she heard her mother's step in the hall. Catrin was carrying the tray with the coffee things. She smiled at them as she moved towards the kitchen, obviously assuming that the reason they were still talking in the hall was because they were loath to part.

Taking advantage of her presence, Gwenyth opened the front door and said, her caressing tone in sharp contrast to the angry colour in her cheeks, 'Goodbye, Jeb.'

His mouth quirked with amusement. 'Goodbye, sweetheart. I'll see you this evening.'

She glared at him, seeing the glint in his eyes that dared her to say when her mother was within earshot that she had no desire to endure his company again today. Holding on to her temper with the greatest of difficulty, she asked, 'What time?'

'I'll call for you around eight.'

He strode off down the drive. She would have loved to have slammed the door behind him. Instead, exercising enormous restraint, she pushed it shut before pivoting and crossing the hall. Smarting from Jeb's arrogant mockery, she needed some time to herself to calm down.

If their relationship had continued on the same sparring note, Gwenyth would have gone on resenting him furiously in the weeks which led up to their wedding. But instead it altered, subtly at first, so that she didn't immediately realise that her emotions were under threat.

It annoyed her to find when she was determined to rile him at every turn that he responded to her barbed comments with masculine tolerance. Even more confusing and annoying was the discovery that, when they weren't clashing, Jeb's sense of humour matched well with hers.

She had believed that she knew exactly what sort of man he was. But she was wrong. For the three years he had lived in Bron-y-Foel, she had deliberately kept a barrier of hostile coldness between them and had seen only his hardness and the steel beneath the charm. But now, as she spent more time in his company, she was beginning to learn that there was a gentler side to his nature that made it difficult for her to hold on to the conception she had of him, stubbornly as she tried to.

Yet, inexorably, her defences were crumbling. She wanted to deny it, but deep down she had always been conscious of the physical attraction he had for her. She had been able to fight that in the past. She might have been able to go on fighting it, had it not been for the crazy sense of rapport she felt with him at times. He seemed able to pick up on her thoughts and mood in a way that was almost uncanny.

They had lingered over coffee after an excellent dinner at a pretty little restaurant in the town, and Jeb was driving her home, when she said, 'You've missed the turn!'

'Are you afraid I'm abducting you?' he teased.

In the glow of the dashboard she caught the gleam of his charismatic smile. It seemed to stop her breathing for a second or two. Feigning an indifference—which she wished were genuine—to his masculine charm, she queried, lightly sceptical, 'Three weeks before the wedding?'

'When you'll be legally mine,' Jeb murmured, a possessive note to his voice as he flicked a glance at her.

The remark was a match to her temper. Coupled with the glow of desire that burned in the depths of his eyes, it sent a hot little shiver tracing over her skin. The prospect of being his wife was beginning to frighten and excite her in roughly equal parts. Not wanting to speculate on her feelings, which were beginning to make less and less sense, she said tartly, 'Do you realise that there are now over a hundred people invited to the reception? I thought you agreed with me that it was to be a quiet wedding.'

'Your father insisted that no expense was to be spared,' Jeb reminded her.

'On the strength of his new job at the quarry,' she said, half to herself, seeing the irony of it.

'Besides, if we'd gone ahead with a small, simple ceremony,' Jeb continued, 'your mother would have been very disappointed.'

'I can't really believe you asked to have the guest-list extended simply to please her, much as the two of you get on well together.'

Jeb considered her remark a moment. Then, as though acknowledging that she had a point, he stated, 'Maybe I'd like you to have the sort of wedding you'll look back on, a magic day to remember always.'

A strange, angry yearning seemed suddenly to tug at her heart. When he spoke that way it sounded as though he loved her. Yet she knew full well that he didn't.

'You've gone very quiet,' he observed, arching a dark eyebrow at her.

'I can't make you out,' she said. 'The only reason you're marrying me is because——'

'I want you,' he supplied, cutting in.

Feeling herself blush, she retorted, 'I do have a mind as well as a body, you know!'

'I never doubted it,' he said, the masculine line of his mouth quirking as he added, 'We have some very intellectual conversations.'

It was a reminder of their discussion over dinner. Somehow they had got talking about the hole in the ozone layer over the Arctic. It had all been most erudite, until she had described how Catrin had once sprayed her hair with furniture polish, mistaking it for lacquer. Jeb had been highly amused by the story.

Refusing to capitulate to his gentle teasing, she asked, as he signalled right, 'Why are we taking the coast road?'

'It's a warm night and there's a lovely moon,' he answered. 'We're going for a walk along the beach.'

The cove where he stopped the car was deserted,

the stillness broken only by the restless call of the sea. Moonlight silvered the massive slopes of the brooding mountains and whitened the sand that had been smoothed free of a single dent or blemish by the tide. The waves rushed shorewards and then retreated to be overtaken by the next breaker, while further out in the vast expense of Cardigan Bay the spuming crests heaved and threshed against the inky blackness of the sea.

Gwenyth's hair blew back from her face in the breeze. It was laced with salt from the sea and she ran her tongue over her lips to taste its tang. The wet sand under her feet scarcely yielded to her light tread.

The immensity and sombre beauty of the sea and landscape seemed for a while to hush her confusion about her feelings. All she wanted was to walk on and on, to drink in the enchantment of the moment, knowing that Jeb's strides were shortened to match hers and that words between them were somehow unnecessary.

They didn't touch. He didn't even take her hand, yet she felt closer to him than she had ever felt before. It was as though they were at one with the sea and the mountains and the dark sky overhead, meant to be as one, now and for all time.

The breeze freshened and she shivered.

'Are you cold?' Jeb asked, drawing her to him.

'A little,' she whispered, her heart lurching.

She slipped her arm around him in return, savouring the warmth and strength of him.

'Do you want to go back?'

'No, let's stay a bit longer,' she answered. 'I like watching the waves roll in.'

Together they strolled up the beach to where the sand gave way to a shelving bank of pebbles.

'Tell me something,' he murmured, when he had enfolded her in his arms so that she was sheltered from the wind as they sat gazing out over the moon-washed sea.

She leaned back against his chest, her thumb dreamily caressing the strong hands that were linked about her waist. It was a wayward interlude, one not to be trusted, one that might look different in the light of day. She told herself all that, but it had no effect on the happy quietness in her heart.

'It depends,' she whispered with a soft teasing smile, 'on what you want to know.'

'What were you thinking as we walked along?'

She coloured slightly and shook her head, refusing to tell him.

'Why not?' he asked.

'Because. . .you might not understand. . .and that would spoil everything.'

'Try me,' he whispered persuasively.

As he spoke he swept her hair away from her neck, pressing his mouth to her nape, while his adroit, knowing hands slid down her soft, shapely arms.

She felt her senses stir feverishly. Her pulse was beating faster and her vision seemed to be narrowing. Oh, no, surely she had more pride than to let him make love to her after the way he had manoeuvred her. Quickly, before the tingling in her blood could grow any stronger, she drew away.

'It's privileged information,' she answered as she got to her feet.

Before he could press her again she kicked off her

sandals to run with unfettered grace over the wet sand towards the sea. Amused, Jeb called after her, 'You're not thinking of a swim, are you?'

She turned, capering a few steps sideways as she called back, bewitchingly elusive, 'No, I'm going to catch the moon in the water.'

Holding her skirt up above her knees, she splashed into the sea. The cold sting of it against her legs made her draw a quick intake of breath. She waded a little deeper, snatching her skirt higher as a wave rushed up, but the moon's silver shivers danced ever out of reach.

She sensed that Jeb was watching her and, after a moment, she heard him tease, 'If you're going to catch anything, it's a chill.'

She turned to make a joking reply, and as a result failed to see the white-topped crest that surged towards her and washed up the back of her thighs, drenching the hem of her skirt.

Hurrying to the shore, she grasped hold of the hand Jeb held out to her and then stumbled in the shallows with a splash. They were both laughing as Jeb hauled her to her feet.

'You idiot,' he said with exasperated humour. 'Look at you, you're soaked.'

She looked ruefully at her drenched skirt. Breathless and laughing, she answered, 'It was your fault I didn't see the wave.'

Chivalrously, he shrugged off his jacket and put it round her shoulders. 'Here, you'd better take this.'

'Thanks,' she said gratefully.

Shivering, she pulled his jacket closer under her chin. It retained the warmth of his body and in it she felt as though she were in his embrace.

'A brandy back at my place should warm you up,' he said. 'I don't want you with pneumonia at the wedding—or was that the idea?'

There was a mocking inflexion in his voice. It shattered the rapport which an instant ago had seemed so real. Anger welled up suddenly inside her as his words reminded her of the harsh reality of their relationship.

Her amber eyes mutinous, she said, 'I've already learned that there's no evading you.'

He grazed a lightly caressing finger down her cheek. 'Do you really want to evade me, Gwenyth?' he asked softly.

At one time she would have flashed back with a quick retort. But now, with her treacherous senses playing her false at every turn, she couldn't immediately answer his question. *Did* she want to escape?

She arched an eyebrow at him, determined that, if she couldn't master the upsurge of panicky confusion she felt, she could at least conceal it. 'Does it matter to you what I want?' she challenged.

The line of Jeb's jaw tightened a little. Glad to see that she had needled him with her defiant answer, she smiled faintly and, as she did so, his eyes narrowed, glinting dangerously.

His gaze still holding hers, he took her chin between his thumb and forefinger, tilting it for her mouth to receive his kiss. Her heart skipped a beat. Caught fast in a web of sexual magnetism, she could only stare up at him, spellbound, as he bent his head.

CHAPTER TEN

BACK at Jeb's house, Gwenyth took a hot shower. The steaming water soon stopped her shivering. She let the jets stream over her skin, wishing she felt less troubled. But that was impossible, when all the time the knowledge was there that soon this house would be her home, the master bedroom, that lay beyond the bathroom door, the one that she would share with Jeb after they were married.

She bit her lip as she remembered the willingness with which she had kissed him on the beach. Until tonight, he had made no attempt to make love to her. It puzzled her as to why that was, especially when the smouldering light she often saw in the depths of his eyes confirmed his desire for her.

Was the reason for his self-restraint the fact that he knew how attracted she was to him? Maybe he was trying to win her by degrees. If so—damn him, he was succeeding!

Hating her vulnerability, she stepped out of the shower and wrapped herself in a large towel. She had agreed to Jeb's terms, and that meant sharing his bed as his wife. Why not just accept the situation? she asked herself angrily. The answer came quickly. When she slept with him, idealistic though the notion was in the circumstances, she wanted it to be an act of love, both on her part and on his.

She went into his bedroom and slipped on his navy silk robe. The caress of the fabric disturbed her, but until her skirt and briefs were dry she had to wear something. She sashed the robe firmly and then, because the sleeves were too long for her, turned back the cuffs.

Brushing her long hair, she went nervously downstairs. Jeb was in the lounge. He had put on a record of Beethoven sonatas and was sitting on the sofa, his long legs stretched out in front of him. Strength and indolent grace were in every line of his relaxed body.

As she paused in the doorway, his masculine gaze swung to her. Instinctively her left hand tightened on the lapels of the navy robe as his eyes made a leisurely appraisal of her.

'Very fetching,' he drawled. 'I've poured you a brandy. Come and sit down.'

'I hope you don't mind, but I've borrowed your hairbrush,' she said, staggered that she could sound so cool and in charge of herself when in every inch of her she was aware of her *déshabillé* and of the static in the air between them.

'You're welcome to borrow anything of mine you like,' he answered.

She took the drink he handed to her, but instead of joining him on the sofa retreated to an armchair.

'Feel safer over there?' he mocked.

She did. Much safer. But, annoyed at the ease with which he seemed to read her, she said, with a touch of her old antagonism, 'You could have driven me straight home.'

A dark eyebrow quirked at her. 'Dripping wet? I'm not planning a late-night seduction scene, if that's what you're afraid of.'

'It wouldn't get you very far if you were,' she told him. 'You don't own me yet.'

'Own you?' he fired back with a frown. 'That's a strange view to have of marriage.'

'How else am I supposed to view our marriage, when you've bought me at the price of saving my father from financial ruin?' she demanded, an angry pain inside her.

'Can't you ever forget that?' he said, an edge to his voice.

'You have to admit,' she said in a cramped tone, 'it's difficult.'

He set his brandy glass aside and got to his feet. 'Then let's suppose for a moment I hadn't forced you into this,' he said as he crossed the room to her.

'What do you mean?' she asked, gazing up at him.

He perched on the broad arm of her chair, his well-cut dark trousers outlining the muscles of his long thighs. 'I'm asking you how you'd feel if there were no pressure on you,' he said.

Her pulse felt the strain as she tried to subdue her awareness of the lean, powerful bulk of him so close beside her. Refusing to give anything away, she answered, as she began to brush her hair again, hair that fell around her shoulders in alluring disarray, 'That's a hypothetical situation.'

There was a short silence. Conscious that a tremor ran through her hand, she went on brushing her hair.

'Let me do that for you,' he said.

'It's all right,' she insisted. 'I'm quite capable of brushing the tangles out myself.'

'Does it bother you, the rapport between us, that suddenly you're putting up barriers again?' Jeb asked lazily.

He was far too perceptive. No longer so certain

that she despised him as much as she claimed, she was wary of every moment of softness between them.

'I wouldn't need to if I felt safe,' she said, and then could have bitten her tongue over what that statement revealed about herself.

'I thought I'd already told you I'm not planning to seduce you tonight,' he replied, the sensual note in his voice quickening her heartbeat. The hairbrush was taken from her hand. 'Sit forward a little.'

The gentle, rhythmic strokes were hypnotic and sensual, increasing her shattering awareness of him. Of late she had been so taken up with trying to sort out *her* emotions that she hadn't given much thought as to what *his* were. But now, as he brushed her hair and the music from the stereo wove magic into the night, she began to wonder.

He had made it very clear that he wanted her, but there was nothing shallow about Jeb. Much as he felt the need to be accepted into the community with a Welsh wife and a Welsh son, she couldn't see him being satisfied with a purely physical relationship.

Losing her grip on reality for an instant, she began, her voice a shade husky, 'Jeb. . .'

'What?' His hand smoothed the curtain of hair he had brushed till it shone like burnished silk.

She turned and looked up into his eyes, which were unfathomable, trying to see the answer to a question it needed courage to ask straight out. But there was nothing in his gaze to suggest anything apart from desire and a trace of amused speculation. Defeated, she stared ahead again and said, 'Nothing.'

'You were going to ask me something. What was it?'

She should have kept her distance from him. That way, this conversation would never have started. Altering what it had been her original intention to say, she asked, 'Have. . .have you ever been in love?'

'What makes you ask that?'

'I wondered. *Have* you?'

'Why this sudden flattering curiosity?'

His voice was laced with mockery. Angry with herself for having been so unutterably stupid as to suppose for even a moment that perhaps his feelings for her ran deeper than he revealed, she snapped, 'Maybe I'd like to know exactly what your relationship was with Lisa.'

'Are you asking me if I'm in love with her?' he jibed gently.

The truth would probably hurt bitterly, but it was preferable to torturing herself with doubts. Holding on to her temper with difficulty, she said, 'You're marrying me because I'm Welsh. For all I know, you might have chosen her if she'd had my Welsh background.'

'Another hypothetical situation,' he mocked.

Her eyes hot and angry, she sprang to her feet, furious with him that he could stir up in her such a blaze of conflicting emotions. 'It's nothing to me whether you're in love with Lisa or not,' she stated stormily, 'but I tell you this. If you ever cheat on me with her after we're married, I don't care what kind of hold you've got over me, I'm walking out on you flat!'

His voice deceptively lazy, Jeb observed, 'You're a passionate little thing when you're jealous, aren't you?'

'This may not be a love-match,' she blazed, 'but I

won't play second fiddle to another woman in your life.'

'You won't have to.'

'What does that mean?' she asked. Having worked herself up into a simmering fury, she felt slightly ridiculous and not inclined to back down. 'Is Lisa important to you or not?'

'I was never in love with her, and she knew that from day one,' Jeb said. 'We enjoyed each other's company in small doses, and that's all there was to it. Any more questions?'

'I'm just trying to understand you,' she said, defending her curiosity. 'We're getting married very soon. Does it surprise you that I'd like us to get to know each other a little better before the great day?'

His gaze travelled over her, lingering on the shadowy hollow of her throat before appreciating her slim legs and then returning to her face again. 'What exactly did you have in mind?' he drawled.

'Not that!' she snapped, thoroughly flustered by now. 'It's hopeless trying to talk to you. I don't know why I bother!'

'It would help if I knew what you were trying to say,' he pointed out.

What *was* she trying to say? She supposed she was sounding him out to see if there was a chance that their marriage would ever be anything other than a calculated contract. And for all her questions she still didn't know. Frustrated and hurting deep down, she said, 'Can't you see that our marriage is never going to work?'

'I have every intention of making it work,' he returned evenly.

'How?' she demanded with exasperation.

'By building on what we already have. We have a lot in common, you and I. We share the same interests, laugh at the same things, and we're very attracted to each other sexually.'

'And you think that's enough?'

'I'd say it augurs for a good marriage with an exciting potential.'

She turned away, hugging herself with her arms and feeling suddenly desolate and very tired. 'I wish I could believe that too,' she said in a forlorn whisper.

She started as two surprisingly gentle hands descended on her shoulders. Pressing a light kiss to her cheek, Jeb said softly, 'Who knows? Maybe in time you'll fall in love with me.'

His words were too ominous for her peace of mind.

Pride made her try to keep up an act of cool hostility towards him when they were alone together, but it wasn't easy when he seemed equally determined to charm her into lowering her guard with him. Just as he knew how to spark her temper, he knew, too, how to fascinate and how to make her laugh.

As her wedding day drew nearer it was small wonder she began to feel more and more on edge and in need of some time to be alone. Just the thought of walking down the aisle to make her vows to Jeb was enough now to throw her into a state of panic.

It was on an evening she had planned to spend quietly at home that she heard the sound of his Range Rover draw to a halt outside on the gravel drive. She'd been about to go upstairs to indulge in a beauty session of manicure and herbal face-mask, therapy she hoped might restore some sense of inner tranquillity.

'That must be Jeb,' she said, surprised that the note of pleasure in her voice had such a genuine ring.

Wasn't it just an act she was putting on for her parents' benefit? Shelving the question, as lately she seemed to be shelving so many that came into her mind about her feelings, she went into the hall to open the door to Jeb.

He was casually dressed in a drop-sleeve, crew-neck sweater in fawn and blue, and navy trousers which emphasised the length of his lean, muscular legs. His gaze slipped over her in its usual appreciative way and her pulse quickened, a reflex response she could do nothing about, however hard she tried.

'What are you doing here?' she began as she stood back to let him in.

'Welcoming as ever,' he mocked. He tilted her chin up. 'You look tired. Are you OK?'

The note of concern in his voice was disarming. 'I didn't sleep well last night. Apart from that, I'm fine.'

He gave her a roguish smile that was unfairly attractive. 'Were you lying awake thinking about me?'

She might have given in to his sense of humour had not his remark hit the nail on the head. On the defensive, she jibed sweetly, 'No, I was weighing up the chances of a reprieve.'

The line of Jeb's jaw tightened a little, but sounding more amused than annoyed by her reply he asked, 'Determined to fight me to the last?'

There were too many sexual overtones in the quip

for her to be able to come back with a second snappy answer. Blushing, she returned to her original question, 'You still haven't told me why you've called.'

'Because I can't keep away.'

She felt a quick stir of temper at the words, which were said ironically. 'I hate insincerity, even when it's flip!'

He smiled at her heated reply, and there was nothing insincere about his tone this time as he observed, 'Do you know that when you're angry there are tiny sparks of gold in your eyes. And when you hide it, as you do sometimes with coolness, you have this way of lifting your lashes slowly that drives me crazy.' His hand traced the line of her face, his gaze shifting to her lips. Brushing them gently with his own, he murmured, 'We're wasting time. I'll just say hello to your parents and then we must get going or we'll miss the start of the film.'

Her heart was beating unevenly, and she took a step back as though hoping some space might protect her from the pull of his dangerous charisma. Sounding not quite as breathless as she felt, she asked, 'What film?'

'I thought we'd drive to Chester, have a quick meal somewhere, and then go to the cinema,' he told her.

She tried to persuade herself that the only reason she had agreed to Jeb's plans without raising any objections was because the film was one she had wanted to see for some time. With a story-line about a woman lawyer who was being terrorised by anonymous death threats, it was a Hitchcock-style thriller and every bit as gripping as the reviews had suggested.

Haunting background music, and low-key camera

work with plenty of shadows, all built up an atmosphere that was so fraught and full of menace that when a downstairs window in the lawyer's house was suddenly shattered in the middle of the night by the butt of a revolver, Gwenyth gasped and clutched Jeb's sleeve.

In the faintly flickering dimness she saw him smile, but even so he took her hand and held it until the tension eased. It was with a strange reluctance that she freed herself as the credits came up on screen.

They came out of the cinema into the cool night air and strolled through the quiet streets to where Jeb had parked the car. He tucked her hand companionably through his arm. She decided it would be unnecessarily wayward to withdraw it.

'I'm glad the film had a happy ending,' she said on a note of contentment.

'You're a romantic,' he teased.

'What's wrong with being a romantic?' she asked, surprising herself with the spontaneity with which she slanted a smile up at him.

'Nothing,' he assured her, smiling back. 'Did you guess at all who was responsible for the death threats?'

She shook her head and admitted with a laugh, 'I invariably suspect the wrong person in thrillers. I wasn't even sure the lawyer's ex-husband was on the level.'

'She wasn't, either. She should have been more trusting.'

'*He* should have been more open.'

Her reply sparked off a joking argument between them that lasted until they reached the Range Rover. She glanced at his strong, chiselled profile as he

unlocked the passenger door for her. In this mood
he was too devilishly attractive. How much longer
could she hope to hold out against his masculine
charisma, and what sort of heartbreak did the future
hold in store if she was ever fool enough to fall in
love with a man who was only marrying her as a
means to an end?

A curious ache beneath her ribs, she leaned her
head back against the comfortable leather seat as he
started the engine. Soon they were driving along the
country lanes, the sweep of the powerful headlamps
silvering the hedgerows.

The purr of the engine and the cosy dimness of the
car interior must have lulled her to sleep, for she
woke with a start some while later as Jeb braked
sharply.

'What is it?' she asked, realising that they were
almost at the head of the pass on the main road to
Bron-y-Foel.

'We've just passed a Ford Sierra,' he answered.
'It's flashing its hazard warning lights and there's a
woman standing by the bonnet looking pretty
helpless.'

Gwenyth turned to glance over her shoulder as he
put the car into reverse. Peering into the darkness,
she said, 'I think she's got a baby with her.'

'Well, if nothing else, we can offer her a lift,' Jeb
said.

The woman ran up to them as they both got out of
the Range Rover. In her late twenties, she was dark-
haired, while the baby she was holding in her arms
was about five months old and crying noisily. She
herself didn't look as if it would take much more for
her to burst into tears with him, as she began, 'I

thought perhaps you weren't going to stop. My car's broken down. Can you help me?'

'What's the trouble with it?' Jeb asked.

The friendly authority in his voice had an immediate calming effect on the woman. Shifting the baby to her other shoulder, she said, 'I don't know. I noticed the temperature gauge going higher and higher as I came up the pass, but I thought that once I got to the top it would be all right. Only then I saw there was steam coming out of the bonnet, so I pulled in. I was afraid to leave the baby in his carry-cot on the back seat in case the engine caught fire.'

'It sounds as if the fan belt may have gone,' Jeb said, opening her car door and ducking into the driving seat to release the bonnet catch.

'Do you think you can get my car started again?' the woman asked anxiously. 'My husband is going to be wondering what on earth's happened to me.'

'I expect I can fix something for you,' Jeb said with his attractive smile.

Observing it, Gwenyth's heart contracted a little. His stopping to help a stranded motorist was the counterpart of his hard business acumen. She'd been too prejudiced against him to see the warm side of his character until recently. Even now it puzzled her. She knew he could be ruthless, and yet he was far from uncaring. To be loved and protected by him. . . She left the thought unfinished. It was far too dangerous to be completed, and she said, 'Here, let me take the baby for you. You look as if you're finding him heavy.'

'Thank you.' The woman smiled her gratitude as she handed her infant son to Gwenyth before following Jeb to the bonnet.

The baby gulped a sob. Seeing that his attention was caught by the beads she was wearing, Gwenyth murmured, 'Do you like these?'

She held the string up. Immediately the baby clutched at it, the crying stopped as if by magic. She smiled at him and then wheeled round in alarm as there was a sudden hiss of steam from the car radiator.

Frowning a little, Jeb stepped back. Wiping his hands with his handkerchief, he said, 'It looks as if it's the radiator hose that's giving trouble. I'll patch it up so the car will get you home, but I'll have to wait till the engine's cooled off a bit more before I can fill your radiator up.'

As he finished speaking his eyes swept over Gwenyth, taking in the baby she was holding with such natural ease. The glance that flew between them didn't need words. She knew exactly what he was thinking, and the telepathy of communication brought a rush of colour to her face. Not so long hence it would be their baby she held in her arms.

Trying to quell the bittersweet emotions that flooded her, she turned away. But it wasn't easy to forget them with the warm little body in her arms. The baby's mother spoke at her elbow, 'What luck for me your husband's good with cars.'

Had she not felt so off balance, Gwenyth would have corrected the woman's assumption. As it was, she allowed her to continue, 'And thank goodness David's stopped crying. Do you have children of your own?'

'No. . .' Her voice was a shade husky and she had to clear it. 'No, not yet.'

'Well, you've got a knack with babies.'

It didn't take Jeb long to get the car started again once the engine had cooled down. Handing the woman her keys and brushing aside her gratitude, he said, 'It should be OK now. Have you got far to go?'

'Only to Cae Afon.'

'In which case you drive off and we'll follow you, though I'm sure the car will get you home all right.'

They followed the Sierra's tail-lights along the darkened road. As it turned off for the village where the woman lived, she tooted the horn lightly and gave them a little wave of thanks.

Gwenyth glanced at Jeb's hands on the steering-wheel as they continued towards Bron-y-Foel. The dark smudges of engine oil made her somehow very aware of the masculine breadth and grace of them.

With stopping to help the driver of the Ford Sierra, it was late, but even so she asked, when ten minutes later the Range Rover drew to a halt outside her house, 'Would you like to come in for coffee?'

'Thanks,' he said, accepting her offer.

Her parents had already gone to bed and the house was quiet. In the kitchen she plugged in the perco-lator while he washed his hands at the sink. The kitchen wasn't small, yet with her senses keyed high, as they always were when he was around, she seemed conscious of his every move.

He turned to pick up the towel, and as he did so she saw the raw mark of a burn across his knuckles.

'You've hurt your hand!'

'It's nothing,' he told her.

'Let me see,' she insisted as she took hold of his wrist. 'It needs some antiseptic cream on it.'

He leaned back against the work-top, watching her

with masculine amusement as she fetched the cream
and a small plaster.

'I'm touched, but there's really no need to play
Florence Nightingale,' he said with humour.

'It will heal quicker if I see to it for you.' She
smiled.

She took hold of his wrist again, hoping he didn't
notice the slight tremor in her hand as she touched
him. She was conscious of his gaze on her, but she
kept hers downcast as she tended to the burn. With
her heart beating a shade unevenly, she tried to
ignore how evocative and taut the silence between
them had become.

Gently she smoothed the cream on to his hand,
noting the dark hairs on his tanned skin. His fingers
were long and dextrous and, she knew from experience, sensitive when it came to caressing.

Finding her voice a little hard to control, she said,
'There. I've finished now.'

He still didn't speak and she glanced up. The nerve
that jumped in his lean cheek showed that he was
every bit as aware of her as she was of him. Their
eyes held, the tense sexual energy that filled the
night with agitation and electricity so powerful that
for an instant she felt almost dizzy.

With sudden intensity he combed his fingers into
her burnished hair. Her lips parted on a soundless,
passionate moan of wanting as they tightened, tilting
back her head.

And then, just as suddenly, she was free again.
Before she had had time to pull herself together Jeb
had reached the door. He turned to say briskly, 'I'll
change my mind about the coffee. It's getting late.'

She clutched hold of the back of one of the kitchen

chairs to steady herself. 'What. . .what did I say?' she faltered in confusion.

His smile was sardonic and didn't abate the glitter in his blue eyes. 'It's not what you say that perturbs me, and you know it. It's everything you do. I don't want coffee. I want to make love to you, fierce, passionate love, and since that's not possible in the kitchen, and under your parents' roof, I prefer to leave before the temptation to disregard all that gets any stronger.'

With that he strode into the hall, leaving Gwenyth in a turmoil, bewildered by the hot stir of desire he could arouse in her and feeling vulnerable and vaguely rejected. Following him into the hall, she caught up with him as he reached the front door. 'Aren't. . .aren't you going to kiss me goodnight?' she asked huskily.

His smile was wolfish. 'So close to our wedding, I'd rather wait for better things.'

Then he was gone. She closed the door behind him and leaned against it. Yet even when his Range Rover had pulled away the night seemed full of static and unrest.

CHAPTER ELEVEN

WITH all the preparations for the church service and the large reception afterwards, the next few days went by in a whirl. Almost before she knew it, Gwenyth was dressed in her bridal gown on the morning of her wedding.

Sian fastened the last tiny button down the back of the closely fitted bodice for her, and then looked up into the mirror. 'Gwen, you look stunning,' she said in an awed voice. 'You'll knock Jeb for six when you walk up the aisle!'

Gwenyth hid her nervousness with the best smile she could manage. Even now Jeb would be sitting in the front pew of the church. His best man would be beside him. In the pocket of his grey morning suit would be the plain gold ring that would proclaim her as Jeb's wife.

As though afraid her courage might desert her, she hurriedly abandoned the train of thought.

'How are we for time?' she asked Sian.

At that moment there was the crunch of wheels outside on the gravel. Hearing it, her sister went over to the window.

'The cars have arrived!' she exclaimed. Turning back to Gwenyth, she went on in a flurry of excitement, 'Do I look all right? Where's my bouquet?'

'It's here on the dressing-table.'

Accepting the spray of pink roses and bud carnations Gwenyth handed to her, Sian said, 'I swear I'm far more nervous than you are, and I'm only the bridesmaid! I don't know how you can be so cool.'

She doesn't know the half of it, Gwenyth thought.

'Sian, dear!' Catrin's voice floated up the stairs. 'The car's here for us.'

'Coming, Mother.' She hurried to the door. Pausing there an instant, she glanced back to say, 'I'll see you in the church porch. I know exactly what to do, so don't worry about a thing!'

The next minute she was gone, with a rustle of lavender silk.

Alone now, Gwenyth turned to look in the full-length mirror at herself. For an instant she caught her breath, scarcely believing the reflection was her own. Straight and slim, the poised young woman in the mirror gave the impression of subtle cameo-sculptured beauty. Her dress, a fantasy of gossamer and white lace, turned her into a vision.

She looked very pale. The pearl choker she wore at her neck, which had belonged to her grandmother, reflected the lustre of her skin. Her amber eyes, thickly fringed by her long lashes, seemed to have a mysterious inner fire of their own, while the cloud of white veil added to her aura of radiance.

Anyone would think I was in love, she thought bewilderedly. But she wasn't. She was determined not to be. Since the announcement of their engagement, she had seen Jeb almost every day. As she had expected, when her family was present he was the ideal fiancé, suave and urbane, using nothing stronger than the weapon of his humour against her even on the occasions when she had done her best to provoke him.

What she hadn't expected was that he would treat

her the same way when they were alone. Perversely, she now wished that he had continued to slash her with his sarcastic mockery. He was forcing her into this marriage. Because of that she wanted to keep the fires of her hatred well stoked, but it was a resolution that had faltered very much of late.

She turned away from the mirror. Her father would be waiting for her downstairs. Feeling strangely calm now that the moment had come, she picked up her bouquet.

With her long train whispering, she walked towards the door. On the threshold she paused. It was the last time she would stand in this room as an unmarried girl, independent and unfettered. When she came back to change into her going-away outfit, she would belong to Jeb Hunter.

To her surprise it was with a certain sadness that she laid aside her bridal gown. She had enjoyed the ceremony and the reception afterwards at her home with the large marquee on the lawn. She looked at her shiny gold wedding ring. It felt strangely right on her finger.

She slipped on her blue and lavender silk suit and, with her bouquet in her hand, descended the stairs. The faces in the hall were uplifted. Smiling, she tossed the bouquet over the banister. There was a swish of skirts and much laughter as one of her friends caught it.

Her mother hugged her, her father squeezed her hand, Sian kissed her cheek and then she was in the car beside Jeb. Confetti was thrown as they drove away and she looked back, a knot of happy emotion in her throat.

Bron-y-Foel was soon left behind as they picked up the road for Welshpool, heading for London. The mood between them remained easy and relaxed until they reached the hotel. It had been a four-hour drive, but Jeb showed no sign of tiredness as he flexed his shoulders before getting out of the car to open her door for her.

With his automatic air of authority he received immediate attention from the girl at the reception desk, who handed him the key to their room. In cream and beige, it was spacious, with all the luxurious touches expected from a world-class hotel, right down to the vase of dusky-pink carnations on the marble-topped dressing-table. Tastefully furnished, it was dominated by the king-sized double bed.

The sight of it made Gwenyth's heart skip a beat. While Jeb tipped the porter who had carried up their luggage, she paced over to the window. Trying to steady her fluttering pulse, she looked out at the commanding view.

Traffic sped along the busy interconnecting roads which converged in the distance on Heathrow. Against the hazy evening sky, a wide-bodied jet dropped height as it came in to land.

They were flying out from the airport the next morning. She still didn't know where to. She had obstinately taken no interest in their honeymoon when Jeb had asked her about it. Subsequently, when he had booked their holiday he had refused to enlighten her about where they were going.

Everyone had sighed at how romantic it was, Jeb whisking her off to some secret honeymoon destination. And she had been forced to smile and agree while her temper had risen under his subtly mocking gaze.

The door closed with a quiet click as the porter went out. Her skin seemed to prickle with the knowledge that she and Jeb were now alone together. Feeling suddenly menaced by the intimacy of the room, she pivoted to face him, defensiveness in every line of her.

Noting it, Jeb's hawkish blue eyes narrowed, his dark brows coming together in a slight frown that made her all the more aware of the strength that was etched in his chiselled features. 'Relax, Gwenyth,' he jibed. 'I'm not about to ravish you.'

'How reassuring,' she said with taut sarcasm.

She tried unsuccessfully to push from her mind the recollection of the poignant moment during the wedding service when she had made her vows to him. It confused her. So did the memory of the laughter they had shared afterwards at the reception, especially now when Jeb no longer seemed the urbane, amusing man she had driven off with amid a shower of good wishes and confetti.

Standing across the room from her, with the double bed between them, he was once again the ruthless foreigner who had always made her feel threatened and who had now coerced her into being his wife. He came towards her, took the clutch-bag she was fidgeting with out of her hands and threw it into an armchair.

'We're ten floors up,' he reminded her drily, 'so it's no good hoping for escape by way of the window.'

'I wasn't thinking of escape,' she told him with hostility.

'No? What were you thinking of, then?'

'Our. . .our wedding.'

She dropped her gaze as she spoke and Jeb prompted, a shading of speculation in his voice, 'What about our wedding?'

Her amber eyes returned to his. What should she say—that despite everything it had seemed like some beautiful dream, that, though she didn't understand it, she had meant her vows when she had said them? She could imagine how that shatteringly honest admission would amuse him.

Hunching her shoulders in a tiny shrug, she moved away. She resumed her study of the view, declining to answer. Jeb came to stand behind her. His hands slid round her slim waist as he drew her back against his powerful man's body.

'Tell me,' he insisted lazily, brushing the nape of her neck with his lips. 'I want to know.'

'Why? What's it to you?' she demanded.

Her hands pushed at his wrists, but instead of allowing her to pull free he turned her in his arms so that she faced him. A strange blend of harshness and mockery in his voice, he said, 'We're married. Husbands and wives are supposed to share their innermost thoughts.'

'They're also supposed to love one another,' she snapped.

'In an ideal world.'

His indifferent reply made her temper flare. The atmosphere was highly charged, but she was in no mood to be cautious. There was a tight ache beneath her ribs, an ache she seemed to have become familiar with of late. Wanting her words to cut, she said. 'You want to know what I was thinking? All right, I'll tell you. I was thinking what an utter farce our wedding was.'

A glint of angry amusement came into his eyes. 'Your parents would be devastated,' he mocked. 'It was the wedding of the year in Bron-y-Foel.'

'Yes, I had everything, didn't I?' she agreed sarcastically. 'The white dress, the Rolls-Royce, the champagne reception. There was only one thing wrong. I didn't get to choose the groom.'

'And you wouldn't have chosen me as your husband?'

'You know damn well I wouldn't!'

'Then more fool you,' he said harshly. 'Because we match each other very nicely. Or have you forgotten?'

Taking hold of her chin with angry fingers, he tilted her head back, his mouth coming down relentlessly on hers. She made a muffled sound of protest as she tried to resist, but Jeb merely tightened his arms around her. Wanting to show her contempt for him, she fought against the treacherous stirrings of desire, losing the battle as Jeb's hands moved to hold her more intimately.

A shock of feverish pleasure went through her. Filled with bewildered desperation, she wrenched herself free, but not before he had sensed her response to him.

'Are you still going to tell me you hate me?' he asked, his voice a shade husky.

She clenched her hands so that he wouldn't see how agitated she was. 'You forced me into this marriage! How do you think I feel?' she flashed stormily.

'Forced, that's a strong word. You could have said

"no" right up to the moment I put my ring on your finger.'

'Could I. And where would that have left my father?'

'You didn't mind letting Marc down,' Jeb pointed out.

'I had no choice.'

'Didn't you?'

'You mean I chose to put my father before Marc,' she said angrily.

'It doesn't suggest you were head over heels in love with him, does it?' Jeb fired back, sarcasm in his voice.

The look she gave him was charged with animosity. She had gradually come to the realisation herself that what she and Marc had shared wasn't strong enough for a lifelong partnership. She had even tried gently to point that out to him when she had written to say that she was returning his ring.

'Perhaps Marc wasn't right for me,' she said stormily. 'But that doesn't mean that you are!'

Afraid that the smouldering tension between them would snap at any moment, she walked past him. Snatching up her clutch-bag, she went into the sanctuary of the bathroom.

Her eyes were dark and dangerously bright, and her throat felt painfully tight. She bit her lip, determined that she wouldn't cry, although her nerves were stretched to breaking-point.

Today at the reception and during the drive to London she and Jeb had seemed to share a sense of rapport, just as they had during the last few weeks of their engagement. But she saw only too clearly now that it had all been an illusion. She must have been crazy to have thought romantically that she could build a loving relationship between them.

A tear traced down her cheek and impatiently she rubbed it away. Jeb was hard and implacable. She was right to hate him. He was ruthless, and if he knew how vulnerable she felt he would only use it to his advantage.

Struggling to keep her emotions, which were far too close to the surface, in check, she neatened her chignon and then touched up her make-up before returning to the bedroom.

Jeb had pulled off his tie and was unbuttoning his shirt. Her heart beating erratically, she crossed over to her suitcase. She had no wish to unpack her things, but she needed to do something to subdue her awareness of him.

'Aren't you changing for dinner?' he enquired.

'I thought I'd wear what I've got on,' she answered, glancing up. 'Do you have any objections?'

'None at all,' he answered, shrugging off his shirt. Her heart seemed to jolt at the sight of his naked chest with its tangle of black hair. 'Your silk suit's very smart and you look good in it. I was merely wondering if you were too embarrassed to undress in front of me.'

There was a shading of humour in his voice, but she was far too on edge to respond to it. Blushing, she lied coldly, 'Of course I'm not embarrassed.'

Jeb's mouth tightened a little. 'Of course not,' he parodied deftly.

'Stop getting at me!' she flashed.

A glint of anger showed in his eyes and she knew that she was taxing his patience. Then, unexpectedly, the harshness went out of his face, and he said almost kindly, 'You've got a bad case of wedding-night nerves, my love. Perhaps dinner and a glass or two of wine will help you to unwind.'

The restaurant, with its intimate lighting and red and gold décor, had the same serene and relaxed atmosphere as the rest of the hotel. It was fairly full, but the unobtrusive teams of waiters ensured that the service was both efficient and solicitous.

To her surprise, she found that she was hungry. The meal, with melon, a chicken dish and the lightest of lemon soufflés, was delicious. Jeb chose a sparkling white wine to accompany it, and afterwards they lingered over coffee.

Without meaning to she gave him a potent look from under her lashes. Something flickered in the depths of his eyes and hurriedly she dropped her gaze, her pulse quickening.

'Lord, you're a witch,' Jeb muttered.

She started slightly as he took hold of her hand across the table. Hurriedly she made to withdraw her fingers from his. But instead of allowing her to do so, he turned her palm over, caressing it lightly with his thumb. Static jumped along her nerves, a tinge of becoming colour staining her cheeks.

His touch was strangely lover-like, and, unable to resist it, she raised her eyes to his. He was watching her with a gentle scrutiny that made her heart lurch. For an instant she couldn't even attempt to marshal her defences against him, the magnetism between them was so strong.

'It's much better when you drop your guard with me,' he said softly.

His words broke the spell and she pulled her hand

away in confusion. She'd tried repeatedly to deny it, but in her heart she knew that her emotions had changed during their engagement. Wishing desperately that his feelings had changed too, she asked, 'Why did you insist on marrying me?'

There was a short silence. She hid her tenseness as she waited for him to answer, while silently she implored him to tell her that he loved her, even if only a little. Instead, he said evenly, 'I thought I'd already explained that.'

'Because you wanted to marry into the community.' There was a trace of bitterness in her voice.

'And because I'm attracted to you,' he answered, 'as you know perfectly well.'

'More so than to any other woman?' she said angrily. 'There must have been many of them!'

Jeb gave her a keen probing look, and immediately she regretted her words.

'Jealous?' he taunted quietly.

'To be jealous I'd have to have some feelings for you,' she said, adding, 'Which I don't!'

'I thought you hated me,' he mocked. Mutinously she didn't answer, and he said lazily, 'It's a heady combination, isn't it?'

'What is?'

'Hatred and passion.'

'I wouldn't know,' she answered, giving him a smouldering look.

The masculine line of his mouth quirked into a brief smile. 'I think we've sat here long enough,' he said. 'Come on, let's make a move.'

His hand against the small of her back, he escorted her from the dining-room. His touch, combined with the thought of their bedroom where the long curtains would now be drawn against the night, made her heart begin to beat unevenly. Quickly she said, 'I'd like a nightcap. I noticed when we crossed the foyer how attractive the bar looked.'

'OK, we'll try it,' he agreed.

The hotel was built round a quadrangle, with the bar she was referring to occupying the central courtyard. Under a vaulted roof of steel and glass, chairs and tables were placed around a lagoon-shaped swimming-pool. Lights flared like blazing torches amid bursts of tropical greenery, while music from a steel band added to the exotic charm of the setting.

She deliberately made her Tia Maria last. Jeb didn't attempt to hurry her. In different circumstances she might have appreciated the canopy of dark sky above and the carefree music, but not with her husband's unsettling gaze on her.

'Can I get you anything else?'

She glanced up as one of the waitresses paused at their table.

'No, thank you,' Jeb spoke for both of them.

The girl took their glasses and moved away.

'You might have asked me first,' Gwenyth protested, flaring unreasonably.

'Are you trying to get drunk?' he asked drily.

'No.'

'To sit up all night, perhaps?'

'I. . . I'm not tired, that's all.'

His blue gaze seemed to caress her. 'Good, because I've no intention of letting you sleep for quite a while yet.'

His intimate words made a hot little shiver trace over her skin. The sensation quickened her temper. Jeb threw her into confusion far too easily, yet how

could it be any other way when he had made it clear
that he intended having her as his wife both in name
and in deed?

'You just can't accept that you leave me cold, can
you?' she snapped.

'You're dead right I can't,' he said softly. 'Now,
are you ready for bed?'

They crossed the wide foyer and took the lift. Its
quietness as it glided up intensified both her nervousness and her anger at the situation she found
herself in. The lift doors slid silently open at the
tenth floor. She walked slightly ahead of him along
the corridor, conscious of his lithe tread behind her.
With her nerves overwrought, more than ever his
footfall reminded her of the measured step of a
hunter.

As part of her trousseau she had bought a bias-cut
nightdress in pale green jacquard silk. Sitting at the
dressing-table brushing her hair while Jeb finished
with the bathroom, she wondered what on earth had
possessed her to choose it. With its tiny shoestring
shoulder-straps and plunging neck and back, it was
far too daring and seductive.

Abruptly she set the hairbrush down and covered
her face with her hands. Suddenly the strain of
knowing deep down that she had fallen in love with
Jeb, yet refusing to acknowledge it, was all too much.

CHAPTER TWELVE

'Gwenyth?'

Jeb's voice startled her. Blinking back tears, she stood up, the pulse that beat at the base of her throat betraying her agitation and distress.

She saw that he was wearing a maroon robe. His legs were bare, and the V between the robe's lapels revealed the tanned column of his throat and the dark curling hairs on his chest. The power of his masculine attraction seemed to strike her like a physical blow, shattering all her carefully constructed defences.

She was conscious of the strength in his face, the dangerous glitter of desire in his eyes as his gaze travelled over her, the sureness in his stance, which belonged to a man who invariably got what he wanted. Unable to hide that she was trembling, she warned in a hoarse whisper, 'Don't. . .don't you come near me! Don't you dare come near me!'

His dark brows drew together with angry impatience. Ignoring what she'd said, he strode towards her, taking hold of her as he demanded harshly, 'What do you think I'm about to do, rape you?'

'Rape or seduction, I don't care what you call it,' she sobbed. 'I'm not sleeping in this room with you!'

'Stop being so hysterical!' he ordered curtly.

'Hysterical. . .you call it hysterical, when I'm in love with you!' she cried, breaking away from him and rushing to the other side of the room. 'I'm not going to give myself to you to satisfy your lust. I was an utter fool to think I could go through with this. But I'm not such a fool as to consummate our marriage knowing that, however much I please you in bed, you don't love me and you're never going to.'

Unable to check the tears that streamed down her face, she threw open the lid of her suitcase, flinging into it the first garments that came to hand.

Jeb stood for an instant as though shocked to the core. The next she felt his hands close on her shoulders as he turned her insistently to face him. There was a hot, leaping light in his dark eyes, but, her vision misted with tears, she failed to see it.

'Leave me alone!' Her voice was choked as her fists came up to hammer at his chest.

Jeb put his hand under her chin, compelling her none too gently to look at him. Scanning her face, he said huskily, 'Not till you say that again.'

'Say. . .say what?' she sobbed, desperately searching her mind for the words he wanted to hear, the words that would make him release her.

His fingers tightened on her chin, his gaze seeming to burn her with its intensity. 'Did I imagine it, or did you just tell me you love me?'

Her heart contracted with a crazy jolt of hope. It wasn't possible that Jeb meant what he seemed to be implying. In a barely audible whisper, she breathed, 'Why. . .why should you care how I feel?'

'You little fool,' he muttered raggedly, his hand dropping to her shoulder. 'Don't you know I'm madly in love with you and have been from the first? Why the hell else do you think I've waited three years for you, manoeuvred you into marrying me rather than risk losing you?'

For a second it was almost too wonderful to comprehend. Her lips parted, a hot glow coming into her eyes. All the tension that had gripped her was suddenly released in a giddy surge of overwhelming joy.

'Oh, Jeb. . .' she whispered, her voice full of emotion, her words all but lost as she met the downward movement of his mouth with eager response.

With a stifled groan he engulfed her in his embrace, kissing her as though he were appeasing the longing of an eternity. Her hands went up around his neck, her lips parting sweetly under his. Jeb's arms brought her even closer to his body, his mouth holding a depth of possessive tenderness that ignited swiftly into desire as she threaded her fingers feverishly into his dark hair.

He lifted his mouth at last, kissing the curve of her neck with an ardent zeal that set her heart thudding. She moaned his name and, as she did so, he raised his head. His eyes were aglitter with passion, but she knew from the gentleness with which he traced his thumb down her cheek that he wasn't going to rush her into bed. With everything certain between them, and the long night ahead, there was ample time for endearments and caresses which would heighten the pleasure for both of them in the moment when he finally possessed her.

'Why didn't you tell me?' she protested, a thread of laughter in her voice as she looked up at him, her amber eyes alight. 'Why did you let me think all you cared about was being accepted?'

'How far would it have got me if I'd told you the truth?' he asked with a smile.

'Which is?' she whispered, wanting to hear him say the magical words again.

'That I'm crazy about you.' He brushed her lips with his, the quiver of restraint she felt in his arms making her pulse quicken. 'I wanted you from the moment I set foot in Bron-y-Foel. But I knew I was going to have my work cut out to win you. My arrival coincided with your father's accident and his leaving the quarry. It was obvious that you blamed me——'

'No, I——' she interrupted.

'Yes,' he insisted. 'It might have been subconscious, but in your mind I was connected with the accident. I thought that, when you came back from your year in France, you would have distanced yourself enough from it to see that none of it had anything to do with me. I hoped you'd stop being so cold with me.' Rueful amusement came into his voice. 'Instead, you came back with Marc. I felt such shock and anger when you told me the two of you were engaged, I don't know how I kept my hands off him. What made it worse was that I saw he wasn't right for you. Yet in a way, too, it made it better. I said to myself, "Lord, she's worth fighting for," and I fought—no holds barred.'

'You certainly did,' she agreed, a smile curving her lips as she remembered his audacity. Lovingly she stroked the lapel of his robe and admitted, 'You made me so angry. And yet I knew I was attracted to you. Just as I knew, though I tried to deny it, that I was jealous when I saw you at the Plas yn Dre with Lisa.'

Jeb's mouth touched the corner of hers. 'She was

never my mistress, if that's what you're thinking. We were only ever friends.'

Very gently and sensuously he bit her earlobe, making her heart skip several beats. With no doubts left in her mind, she wanted nothing more than to succumb to the feverish sensations which were heating her blood.

'Love me,' she whispered huskily.

'Lord, you enchant me, Gwenyth,' he muttered, the words almost wrenched from his throat.

Her arms wound around his neck as, with a low growl, he swept her off her feet and carried her to the large double bed. He laid her on the covers, kissing her deeply as he joined her, his mouth searching and demanding as though she intoxicated him. His hands caressed her, stroking the warm skin of her back, making a melting, exciting pleasure race through her whole body.

She shivered and, as she did so, he raised his head. His breathing coming hard, he murmured, 'I've wanted to kiss you and love you like this from the very first moment.'

He slipped the thin straps of her nightdress down over her shoulder, his lips tracing the curve of her breast. She moaned as he caressed her, her hand sliding inside his robe. As though impatient to have no barrier between them, he shrugged it off, pressing her breasts to the hard plane of his hair-roughened chest as he kissed her again with a deep, raw passion.

She trembled as she felt his weight, a feverish excitement driving her to touch and explore the lean perfection of his naked body. The muscles of his back and shoulders were hard and firm, and to add to her delight she sensed a shudder go through him as her fingers ran down his spine.

He bent across her, girdling her waist with his kisses before pushing her hair off her face to slide his mouth along the line of her jaw and down her throat. His powerful body seemed to be enveloping her. She turned her head feverishly against the pillow, responding to him with a sexuality she had scarcely known she possessed.

The waves of wanting that were coursing through her became still fiercer, making her tremble. She felt that she couldn't bear it, Jeb was arousing her to a pitch of pleasure so agonising and intense.

On fire for him to take her, she arched against him. And then her fingers dug into his back, her choked sob drowned by Jeb's growl as he entered her. Her eyes flew open to meet the dark, driving passion in his, the slight pain of his first penetration lost in the dazzling beauty of union with him.

The storm of sensation gathered, and she closed her eyes tightly again as she moved with him, until suddenly the unbearable pleasure seemed to explode throughout her whole body. She tensed and cried out. Jeb's shuddering groan of fulfilment came at the very instant her teeth cut into his shoulder.

Afterwards she lay spent and unmoving. Her heart was thudding and she could still feel the ripples of response echoing through her. Dazed by the force of what she had experienced with him, she drew a deep, unsteady breath and, as she did so, Jeb moved to lie beside her.

He drew her into his arms with infinite tenderness, enchancing the magic of all that had gone before as his hand caressed her slim back. She felt as if their union had shattered some golden store of nectar deep within her, and now, as he cherished her in love's afterglow, it flooded her body with a sweet sense of exhaustion and peace.

'Mine at last,' Jeb said softly. 'Are you happy, sweetheart?'

'Wonderfully so,' she whispered.

'I didn't hurt you?'

'No. Or at least if you did it was only momentary. You were so very gentle.'

Jeb caught hold of her fingers and pressed his lips to her palm. 'Then it was perfect for both of us,' he murmured.

She smiled, resting her cheek against his chest and feeling the strong, even beat of his heart. The contentment that enveloped her was deeper than anything she had ever known before, the prospect of their honeymoon filling her with a glow of happiness.

'Do you think you could let me into a secret?' she asked.

Jeb propped himself up on an elbow and looked down at her. Brushing a strand of burnished hair away from her face, he said, 'I have no secrets from you.'

'You do. You haven't told me where we're going on our honeymoon.'

'How do you feel about Madeira?' he murmured. 'Flowers, sunshine and warm, starry nights.'

'It sounds like a dream!'

She linked her arms around his neck and kissed him. When at last he raised his head they were both smiling.

'And I thought you only wanted to marry me to get a son,' she said, laughter in her voice.

'I married you because I love you. I hope we will have children, but there's plenty of time.'

'Not really. Not if you want four.'

He gave her a look of puzzled amusement. 'Four? What gave you that idea? Not that I've any objections,' he said, nibbling her ear.

'So you don't know everything about Welsh love spoons,' she teased.

'I knew enough to win you with one, but enlighten me. What else did I tell you with it?'

'The carving on the stem showed four wooden balls. They're supposed to denote the number of children the man hopes to have.'

'What did you do with the spoon?' he asked.

'I kept it.'

'Then we must give it pride of place above our bed.'

For an instant she imagined the children they would have. Then his hand moved to caress her breast, sending a quicksilver quiver of desire through her. Her gaze locked with his, the glitter of passion and love she saw in his eyes telling her that the same fever ran in his blood as in hers.

Tantalisingly and slowly, he drew her back with him into the enchanted world of desire, a world that held all the promise and beauty of the future.

Zodiac Wordsearch
Competition

How would you like a years supply of Mills & Boon Romances ABSOLUTELY FREE?

Well, you can win them! All you have to do is complete the word puzzle below and send it into us by Dec 31st 1990. The first five correct entries picked out of the bag after this date will each win a years supply of Mills & Boon Romances (Six books every month - worth over £100!) What could be easier?

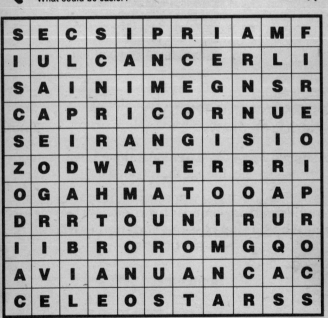

S	E	C	S	I	P	R	I	A	M	F
I	U	L	C	A	N	C	E	R	L	I
S	A	I	N	I	M	E	G	N	S	R
C	A	P	R	I	C	O	R	N	U	E
S	E	I	R	A	N	G	I	S	I	O
Z	O	D	W	A	T	E	R	B	R	I
O	G	A	H	M	A	T	O	O	A	P
D	R	R	T	O	U	N	I	R	U	R
I	I	B	R	O	R	O	M	G	Q	O
A	V	I	A	N	U	A	N	C	A	C
C	E	L	E	O	S	T	A	R	S	S

Pisces	Aries	Leo	Earth	**Please turn over for entry details**
Cancer	Gemini	Virgo	Star	
Scorpio	Taurus	Fire	Sign	
Aquarius	Libra	Water	Moon	
Capricorn	Sagittarius	Zodiac	Air	

How to enter

All the words listed overleaf, below the word puzzle, are hidden in the grid. You can can find them by reading the letters forwards, backwards, up and down, or diagonally. When you find a word, circle it, or put a line through it. After you have found all the words, the left-over letters will spell a secret message that you can read from left to right, from the top of the puzzle through to the bottom.

Don't forget to fill in your name and address in the space provided and pop this page in an envelope (you don't need a stamp) and post it today. Competition closes Dec 31st 1990.

Only one entry per household (more than one will render the entry invalid).

Mills & Boon Competition
Freepost
P.O. Box 236
Croydon
Surrey CR9 9EL

Hidden message _____

_____

Are you a Reader Service subscriber.   Yes ☐   No ☐

Name_____

Address_____

_____

_____

_____ Postcode_____

COMP9